"Hold still," he said in a low growl. "Raven, stop fighting me."

He'd cuffed her wrists, but it was his voice more than his action that stilled her.

His hair brushed her cheeks, and she could almost make out the details of his features in the light that filtered through the high window. She added in the scent of his skin—frighteningly familiar—the shape of his muscles, the feel of his body against hers, and…

Already racing, her heart knocked into her ribs. She couldn't speak or move, was half-afraid to breathe as she stared into his eyes.

Planting her palms on his chest, she shoved him back far enough that she could scramble to her hands and knees. Heart slamming, she confronted his shadowed silhouette.

"You're a lie," she accused. "You're not here. You can't be—" the denial turned to dust in her throat "—here."

JENNA RYAN

STRANGER ON RAVEN'S RIDGE

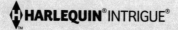
HARLEQUIN® INTRIGUE®

For Alice, Jim and Laurie:
You never say goodbye to someone you love.
The loved are always alive in our hearts.

ISBN-13: 978-0-373-69678-9

STRANGER ON RAVEN'S RIDGE

Copyright © 2013 by Jacqueline Goff

Recycling programs for this product may not exist in your area.

This edition published by arrangement with Harlequin Books S.A.

For questions and comments about the quality of this book, please contact us at CustomerService@Harlequin.com.

® and TM are trademarks of Harlequin Enterprises Limited or its corporate affiliates. Trademarks indicated with ® are registered in the United States Patent and Trademark Office, the Canadian Trade Marks Office and in other countries.

Printed in U.S.A.

www.Harlequin.com

ABOUT THE AUTHOR

Jenna started making up stories before she could read or write. As she grew up, romance always had a strong appeal, but romantic suspense was the perfect fit. She tried out a number of different careers, including modeling, interior design and travel, but writing has always been her one true love. That and her longtime partner, Rod.

Inspired from book to book by her sister Kathy, she lives in a rural setting fifteen minutes from the city of Victoria, British Columbia. It's taken a lot of years, but she's finally slowed the frantic pace and adopted a West Coast mind-set. Stay active, stay healthy, keep it simple. Enjoy the ride, enjoy the read. All of that works for her, but what she continues to enjoy most is writing stories she loves. She also loves reader feedback. Email her at jacquigoff@shaw.ca or visit Jenna Ryan on Facebook.

Books by Jenna Ryan

HARLEQUIN INTRIGUE

393—SWEET REVENGE
450—THE WOMAN IN BLACK
488—THE ARMS OF THE LAW
543—THE STROKE OF MIDNIGHT
816—EDEN'S SHADOW
884—CHRISTMAS RANSOM
922—DREAM WEAVER
972—COLD CASE COWBOY
1027—MISTLETOE AND MURDER
1078—DANGEROUSLY ATTRACTIVE
1135—KISSING THE KEY WITNESS
1182—A PERFECT STRANGER
1227—SHADOW PROTECTOR
1259—DARKWOOD MANOR
1298—DAKOTA MARSHAL
1346—RAVEN'S COVE
1411—STRANGER ON RAVEN'S RIDGE

CAST OF CHARACTERS

Raven Blume—Two years after her husband's death, she's thinking of moving to her ancestral home.

Aiden McInnis—He faked his death to save his wife, Raven's, life.

George Parkins—Aiden's double-dealing friend wants Raven—at any cost.

Reverend Alley—The mysterious fanatic is not the person he claims to be.

Johnny Demars—The cruel crime boss has an agenda—and one very big secret.

Fergus Smith—He keeps turning up where he's not supposed to be.

Weasel—The hired killer has more than death on his mind.

The "Big Guy"—He stays in the shadows until the last minute.

Steven Blume—A disbarred lawyer, Raven's cousin is desperate for money.

Great War did end, returning home, so many wounded souls,

Could not shut out what they had seen, and done, did not feel whole.

To Maine and Raven's Cove they came, to convalesce as one.

They did not know, they were not told, the truth, what had been done,

By man and evil spirit, joined together, roaming free,

No war could match a man possessed, for sheer brutality.

When man was transformed into bird, the Raven's Tale was born.

The evil could no more hold sway, Cove dwellers need not mourn,

Until the soldiers came to stay and one among them learned.

His brother had been murdered by a friend. That friend would burn,

In Hell's own fire, the soldier vowed, and left the hard fought path.

He let the evil seed take root inside him, let his wrath,

And bitterness and hatred grow. Forgiveness held no place,

Inside his broken mind or heart. There was no room, no space,

For any thought not gripped by evil's dark and binding claws.

He killed his friend and threw the body from the ridge, then paused,

Drew one last breath and shouted from the ridge up to the sky.

"The deed is done, my loss avenged, an eye plucked for an eye."

The soldier ended his own life that night in blinded grief.

But nothing of the evil died, there was no such relief.

For those who think to pass through Raven's Cove without a care.

Take heed, recall this tale, resist the darkness. And beware.

Chapter One

Aidan McInnis craved a foot-long sub, fully loaded. And a Coke. Well, a beer really, but he was driving, and his police partner, Len Gaitor, was not only fully loaded, but currently weaving his way down the aisle of Pop Daly's ancient Stop 'N Shop. Their friend, George Parkins, had fallen asleep in the backseat of Aidan's truck half an hour ago.

Overstocked and understaffed, the small store smelled of stale coffee and nacho cheese. Just south of two in the morning, it also carried the unmistakable scent of the marijuana one or both of the clerks had probably just smoked in the john.

Not his problem, Aidan thought, heading for the sandwich section. He and his friends were off duty tonight

They'd watched the Brewers take apart the Pirates, then switched it up and checked out a handful of UFC matches in a backstreet venue whose operation was at best half-legal. But Aidan had drawn the line at the stripper bar Gaitor had suggested after that. Hey, barely twenty-four months married to a woman like Raven, even a detective of ten plus years could say no without hesitation.

The out-of-sight door jangled as another customer entered. Aidan heard a squelch of rubber while his gaze explored the piss-poor selection of subs. The store was half a century old and in need of a major renovation. But Pop being a major tightwad wouldn't lift a finger until the cash flow—substantial due to location—dropped off.

"Only got light beer left." Gaitor grumbled his way to Aidan's side. "Can't keep a buzz on drinking damn soda pop. Your wife's in Minnesota until Wednesday, McInnis. Let's find us a girlie bar."

Aidan ran his gaze over the display again. Pathetic. "Gotta work tomorrow, Gaitor."

His partner snorted. "Night shift. And me a few months from retirement. It's a kick in the ass by an ass of a captain. I hate it when yes-men brownnose their way to the top."

No surprise there, Aidan thought in mild amusement, since Gaitor hated pretty much everything to do with police work these days.

He was about to downgrade his sub craving to a slightly more palatable ham and Swiss on rye when he caught the angry command up by the cash register.

Gaitor heard it, too, and scowled. "Wouldn't you just frigging know it. Stupid punk needing cash for a fix is hell-bent on screwing up my night. Talk about your bad timing."

Aidan drew his Glock from the shoulder holster under his jacket. "Kids behind the desk'll probably consider it good. I'll take the rear."

Gaitor patted his chest and sides. "Musta left my gun in the truck."

Maybe lucky for the thief, Aidan reflected, and left his partner muttering in the aisle.

He spotted the new arrival instantly, a lone male wearing a gray hoodie and ski mask. The 9 mm in his double-fisted grip was pointed at the forehead of the older store clerk. Less than two feet from his target, he was unlikely to miss if he squeezed the trigger.

The clerk gaped, openmouthed. "We don't keep—I mean—there's no money." His hand fumbled for the cash drawer below. "Pop's rules. Nothing bigger than a twenty after ten o'clock."

"Open it," the thief ordered.

He sounded tight—a little edgy and a lot mad. High was a given. Meth or crack, Aidan assumed.

The old-fashioned drawer pinged as it sprang outward. In the shadows, Aidan took aim.

"There's only fifteen bucks." The clerk's Adam's apple bobbed. "See for yourself."

Aidan saw the thief's teeth in profile. One step forward, and he'd have him.

"Lift the tray out."

"But Pop won't—"

"Lift it!" the thief snapped. His gun hand shook, and his breath heaved in and out. "You don't do what I tell you, more than your night's gonna be over."

"Stop right there," Aidan said from slightly behind him.

The masked head jerked around. For a moment, nothing and no one moved.

"I'm a cop," Aidan warned. "And I'm guessing I'm a helluva lot better shot than you."

The thief started to lower his arms. Then the floor creaked, and he snatched them up again. He fired wide twice, and twice more with better aim. The clerks vanished behind the counter.

Aidan went for the right arm. It should have been an easy hit. But in a lightning-quick move, the thief leaped sideways and exposed his full chest. Aidan's bullet struck him at the same instant the thief's bullet embedded itself in a tall shelf. The man took two staggering steps forward. And dropped like a stone to the floor.

At the entry door, George Parkins stood with an owlish expression on his face that suggested he had no idea where he was.

Gaitor lurched into sight. With his eyes locked on the fallen man, he used his toe to nudge an unmoving arm. "Who'd have figured he'd pull a dumb-ass stunt like that. Bastard couldn't have hit you in a million years."

Aidan glanced at the bullet hole six inches from his head and wasn't so sure.

"Uh, what...?" was the best George seemed able to manage.

The younger clerk stared, pop-eyed. "Is he dead?"

"As a doornail," Gaitor confirmed. He withdrew his fingers. "You had no choice, Aidan. You couldn't have known he'd turn."

"Are you hurt?" Aidan asked the older clerk.

"Yes—I mean no, not bad. He—he got my arm a little."

Aidan made a head motion at George who was alert enough to duck under the pass-through.

"It's a flesh wound." George squinted as if through a fog. "Bullet didn't penetrate. I'll call it in."

"You saved my life." The injured clerk's voice trembled. "He was gonna do me for following Pop's stupid rules."

The eyes of the thief, already glassy, stared upward from the scarred linoleum floor. His mouth sagged open. Aidan tugged off the ski mask that covered his face.

And, closing his own eyes, he swore long and full.

"What?" Gaitor demanded. Then he looked down, and his shoulders drooped. "Jason Demars. Hell."

Close, Aidan decided. Dangerously close.

Thoughts spiraled through his head. But the one that stood out, the one that intensified as it repeated again and again and again was simple and concise.

He was a dead man.

Milwaukee, Wisconsin
Twelve days later.

"IT WAS MY FAULT." George Parkins rocked back and forth on the creaking church floor, ten feet from a wreath of white lilies. "I should have gone into the store sooner, but I drank too much and passed out in the backseat of Aidan's truck." He stopped rocking to clutch at Raven Blume's arms. "Johnny Demars's men will come for me and Gaitor now. Demars is all about revenge. It's his way, and Jason was his son, his only kid. Doesn't matter there's no hard evidence, we know it was him who did Aidan. Blew him to hell in pieces. It had to be him."

When George's grip faltered, Raven slipped free. Maybe some part of this nightmare would register later, but for the moment, very little of it, including, thankfully, the pain, penetrated the wall of shock that stood between her and grim reality.

Aidan, her husband of two short years, was dead. It didn't sound real even when she thought the words. But George was right. Aidan had been blown to hell in pieces six days ago. Blown there from the inside of a condemned movie theater. The resulting fire had blazed so hot it had consumed everything, human, rodent and insect, trapped within it.

Captain Beckett said Aidan had made plans to meet an informant in the lobby. No one knew the informant's identity, or if he'd been blown to hell, as well. However, strong speculation was that the explosives had been set by Johnny Demars himself. Which was absolutely possible since no one, except perhaps his late son, had any idea what the crime lord looked like.

Beckett had refused further comment, but everyone in the loop recognized Demars's name. They also knew just how vindictive he could be. Especially where his son was concerned.

Beside her, George continued to talk, but his words were a weird babble in Raven's head. Surreal. Like the hundreds of faces swimming in front of her.

Two of those faces belonged to Aidan's grandparents, the people who'd raised him. Her own parents had flown in from Illinois. And of course there was the tragic face of Aidan's police partner. Mere months from retirement, Len Gaitor blamed himself for Aidan's death even more than George did.

"I was right there in the store when Jason tried to rob it. I should've been there when Aidan…" His fingers closed around the arms Raven had just succeeded in freeing. "We were partners. A good partner would have gone to that theater with him."

He continued to talk, wouldn't let her go.

Maybe it was just as well, Raven thought, because she'd been floating more than standing all day, and the ordeal was far from over.

The wreath that surrounded Aidan's headshot photo was going to be transported to McGinty's Bar downtown for a full Irish wake, as per the wishes of his grandparents.

Aidan had been born in Dublin to a pair of restless world travelers. They'd died before his fifth birthday. Afterward, he'd gone to live with his grandfather and grandmother McInnis in New York City.

The cop thing had been in his blood forever. Sadly, while Raven had always been aware that the meaning of *forever* could change radically on any given shift, she hadn't expected it to be so abrupt. Or so final.

"Everyone who knows the name knows it was Demars who did this." Gaitor gave Raven a shake that had nothing to do with her and everything to do with his own self-directed anger. "I knew he'd be out for blood. I should have dogged Aidan from dawn to dusk to dawn."

"You or me." Eyes glazed, George resumed his grieved rocking.

From her vantage point near the side wall, Raven watched Captain Beckett and Aidan's grandfather herd the crowd of mourners toward the front doors. In the background, Aidan's grandmother clung to her rosary and sobbed.

Friends and family paused to offer heartfelt condolences. Raven shored up her wall and acknowledged them, or hoped she did, with grace and gratitude.

The church fell silent. The shadows deepened. The setting changed from stoic cemetery to noisy Irish bar.

There were people everywhere. Laughing, crying, eating, drinking. Recalling. Recounting.

Gaitor huddled in a dark corner with a bottomless glass of whiskey and brooded. George, eyeglasses askew, danced with Aidan's grandmother. Raven's mother made sure everyone was fed well. Her father philosophized with anyone who'd listen. McGinty poured drinks and shouted some tidbit of information about her great-grandfather, Rooney Blume, who was his oldest and most colorful friend.

An angular woman in a black dress, with lines of strain around her mouth, offered Raven a smoked salmon canapé from a silver tray. A potbellied man in a plaid jacket offered her a puppy from his new litter. A young man with stringy brown hair played the fiddle onstage, while another, hairy as a werewolf, accompanied him on a wheezy accordion.

The bar was dim, and her head filled with smoke. A thick gray cloud of it that, like the wall, held the worst of the pain at bay.

Words flowed and, with them, an abundance of liquor. The drink loosened tongues and made those words slightly less guarded.

"How dreadful for you, a doctor, not to be given a chance to save your husband's life," a burly woman slurred. Raven thought she might be a desk sergeant from a cross-city precinct. "Aidan was a good man, a good cop. Totally hot." She set her arms on Raven's shoulders, leaned in and winked. "So totally damn hot you could scorch your eyeballs looking at him."

Yes, Raven thought, *you could. Or could have. An aeon ago when he'd been alive.*

A thin whip of pain snaked into her heart. She felt her face go white.

Gaitor came up behind her. She recognized him by the combined smell of whiskey and drugstore cologne.

The scent gave way to smoked salmon as the server in black returned to press more canapés on her. In a stern, no-nonsense tone, she told Raven that starving herself would not bring her husband back. She knew that for a fact because she'd gone through a similar trauma when her husband had died more than a decade ago.

Raven merely smiled, nodded and ate the canapé. Nudging the tray aside, Gaitor steered her to a vacant rear table.

As she drifted through the music and shadows, Raven's life with Aidan played like a newsreel in her head.

The detective and the doctor, living the Bohemian life-style in a third-floor walk-up.

Her intern hours had sucked. His alternating weekends and night shifts had made time together a rare and precious thing. That was in the early days of their relationship, when the sex had been stupendous and everything they'd done had been a magical mystery tour.

They'd sailed around Lake Michigan for three weeks with friends. Later that summer, they'd ridden not-quite-trained horses on a colleague's ranch. They'd white-water rafted in Idaho and watched the worst ever off-Broadway play in a theater with a crippled AC system during a wicked August heat wave.

Then, on a glorious September afternoon, a year and half after they'd met, they'd gotten married. They'd actually stolen two full weeks away from crime and medicine for an amazing honeymoon in Tuscany.

Aidan had rented a castle, complete with staff. They'd made love—still stupendous—drunk wine and, to Aidan's amusement, wangled a cooking lesson from a ninety-year-old woman who didn't speak a word of English.

Two weeks had turned into two years. Just. Then she'd gone to Minnesota. Aidan, George and Gaitor had gone to a baseball game, and Jason Demars, nowhere near the phantom his father was, had decided to rob Pop Daly's Stop 'N Shop.

Aidan had understood the need to watch his back after Jason's death. So had Captain Beckett, who'd watched it even more rigorously. But cops like Aidan always had active case files. So when one of his more reliable informants had called him with a tip on a major homicide, Aidan had gone to meet him. Alone, as was his habit.

The informant might have been paid off by Johnny Demars. He might have been misinformed. Whatever the case, Raven knew the derelict theater had long been Aidan's meeting place of choice.

"You need to sit down now." Gaitor pressed her onto a leather bench. "I'll get you a glass of brandy. That'll do the trick."

It would do something, Raven thought, though probably not what he anticipated.

The music changed from Irish jig to Irish lament. Through the haze in her head, a picture of Aidan came clear. He'd been quintessentially black Irish, tall, lean boned and gorgeous, with black hair and almost black eyes. There'd always been a hint of dark stubble on his face because—well, because polished had never been Aidan's style. He'd stuck to jeans and Ts, work or biker boots and, as a rule, some form of leather jacket. His hair? Grown a little long and more often than not, left to wave a little messily around his striking face.

"McGinty thought whiskey would do you better." Sitting, Gaitor pushed a glass, three fingers high, into her hand. "He tells me it's a family favorite."

And since McGinty also had a lot of family in Raven's Cove, Raven expected he would know.

With Aidan's image still front and center, she brought the glass to her lips, waited a beat, then shot all three fingers.

It was pure, liquid fire, a blazing line of it that decimated the wall and blew a wide hole in the smoke.

For six nightmarish days, Raven had been in shock. Nothing and no one had touched her emotions. Couldn't, because the wall had been there to hold them in. Once it vanished, the pain literally erupted.

Aidan was dead. The only man she ever planned to love was gone. Forever. That wasn't pain; it was devastation.

Her eyes came into sudden, sharp focus on Gaitor's. She saw the sheen of tears inside them. And for the first time in six eerily long days, she broke down and wept.

Chapter Two

"YOU'VE LOST YOUR mind. I mean it. You are deep in the woods with no bread crumbs, heading straight for the gingerbread house." George Parkins dug in and held on as Raven downshifted the small cube van to navigate a steep slope. "This is crazy. You're on track to be a top-flight diagnostic physician. You're moving and shaking—and I'm not referring to this rattletrap truck you rented. What on earth made you listen to a man five decades older than Methuselah and put a to-die-for job on hold? And please don't say so you could practice medicine in the speck of a town where Methuselah's grandfather lives."

Raven kept her eyes on the thin slice of road that probably hadn't seen a paving crew since Elvis's time. "Methuselah's grandfather is my great-grandfather, George. His name's Rooney Blume."

"And he's in possession of how many faculties?"

"More than you and me combined, I imagine." She sent him a quick grin. Very quick. The pothole she'd avoided a moment ago could have passed for a wading pool. "Raven's Cove needs a doctor. The population tops a thousand these days, and all they have physician-wise is a retired army medic with so-so vision and a lingering case of shell shock. That won't provide much comfort to a woman in her third trimester or a man with a ruptured hernia. Besides—" she downshifted again "—you volunteered to ride shotgun. No one's asking you to live here."

George offered back a strange look. "So you've decided to make the move, then? I'd hoped you were only doing a favor for an old man."

"I am—for now. Rooney needs new appliances, and the friend from whose small store he made his purchase can't deliver them. I wanted to check out Raven's Cove, the drive's manageable even in a rattletrap truck, and I like doing favors for friends and family. Especially for one very old man who's optimistic enough to believe he'll be able to enjoy a kitchen full of new appliances well into the next decade."

With a baffled shake of his head, George regarded the sky. "Are those purply-black things up there rain clouds?"

Raven avoided a deep rut. "My mother says they're a perpetual formation at this time of year."

"Uh, okay… Do I want to know why?"

A teasing smile appeared. "It's part of an ancient legend. Involves one of my ancestors. Said ancestor, Hezekiah Blume, allowed an evil spirit to take possession of his soul. He thought better of it later, but couldn't wriggle out of the deal without major help. Enter a good spirit who tried and failed to exorcise its nasty counterpart. The only option left was transformation. Man and evil became a raven."

"So you're…are you telling me you were named for a legend?"

"In a way. But only if you want to be technical, which my mother hasn't been since the day she was born. They called her Spacey Lacy when she lived here."

"Who are they?"

"Acquaintances mostly, many of whom have absolutely no business throwing stones since the bulk of them believe that any person finding three raven's feathers on their door is destined to die."

"Raven's feathers," George repeated. "On the door."

"Placed there by the clairvoyant raven into which Hezekiah was transformed."

George stared at her. "When did this transformation take place?"

"Three centuries ago, give or take."

"So we're talking about one freaking old bird."

"If you believe, yes. Otherwise, it's just a bread crumb and gingerbread tale." Her lips twitched at his befuddled expression. "I did warn you before you flew to Portland that Raven's Cove was a little odd, and you might want to rethink your decision to come."

When his features softened, Raven sighed a little. Despite the distance between Milwaukee and Rochester where she now lived, George had been coming on to her for the past twelve months, in his own quiet way. She'd been able to sidestep his advances to this point, but it occurred to her now that his being in Raven's Cove, even for a few short days, might prove—tricky. And the twinges of guilt she'd been experiencing lately didn't help.

Before her conscience could get the better of her, she motioned at a structure coming into view through a dense stand of woods.

"There it is. Blume House. Hezekiah's pride and joy. Until he slid into a funk and went all evil host on his friends and family."

George's bespectacled eyes widened as the house grew in size. "It's like a Black Forest castle."

"Back in the day—in Germany where it was originally built—it was a fortified manor house. Aidan and I came here once." Although the pain still sliced deep, Raven pushed through it and continued. "It was before we were married, a few short weeks before a storm took out half the west wing. My cousin Riese was running the place as a hotel at the time. Then *whoosh, bang,* along came Hurricane Enid, down came a bunch of walls, and that was the end of it for Riese. She covered the furniture, locked the doors and struck out for Palm Springs with a cop she'd met several months earlier. The house has been vacant for the past five years."

"Looks like it's been vacant for the past five decades."

Raven eased the truck to a halt outside a set of rusting iron gates fashioned into the silhouette of a raven.

George's gaze glued itself to the gothic-style house behind them. "You're considering setting up a medical clinic here in—I'm sorry, I have to say it—spook central?"

"I am, unless the hurricane damage is more extensive than Rooney claims." Raven banded her arms around the steering wheel and leaned forward to look. "It's a rejuvenating prospect, a sea change from the work I've been doing in Minnesota."

"At the Mayo Clinic, Raven. That's one pretty desirable work place."

"Venue doesn't matter. That I'd be doing something more community oriented does. Losing Aidan…" The breath she drew threatened to choke her, but she persevered. "Losing him took me out of my orbit for a long, long time. I'm not back in it yet, not all the way in it, but I know what I need to do, and that's something vastly different from what I've been doing for the past two years. Routine's a balm, but according to my mother and

Rooney, I've only been existing since Aidan's funeral. They want me to rejoin the living."

George's gray eyes sobered. "I could help you with that, you know."

She took care with her expression and her tone. "You did, and you are. Believe me, George, if I could…" She halted to twist in her seat and peer down the road.

Unsure, George mimicked the move. "What?"

"I don't know. A feeling. Probably nothing." But she couldn't stop the shiver that chased itself over her warm skin. "This might sound weird—and for 'weird' read 'paranoid'—but I keep thinking there's someone behind me. Following me, maybe watching me. Closely and with intent."

"Like a Peeping Tom?"

"More like a shadow."

"Or a ghost?"

From under the bill of her Brewers cap, Raven slid her narrowed eyes to his face. "I'm not channeling Aidan. This is a legitimate intuitive feeling. And yes, I know those terms contradict each other. I also know Captain Beckett hasn't been really easy about things since Gaitor dropped off the radar twenty-plus months ago."

Worry invaded George's features. "He's not alone. Last I saw of Gaitor, he was heading out with a six-pack and a loaded sub. 'Homage to Aidan,' he told me. Then he got in his crappy little car and drove home to watch a football game. That was a week after his retirement party. Since then, there's been no sign of him. He gave up his apartment without notice and vanished. It's like the ground swallowed him whole. He even left his car behind."

Raven tried not to let her skin crawl. People did strange things. Gaitor didn't owe her or anyone an explanation for his behavior. Assuming his disappearing act had been behavioral, and not a belated shot fired by a still-seething and not-yet-sated crime lord.

Cheery prospect, she reflected and gave the bill of her cap a tug. Hopping out, she stretched her arms upward to relieve the ache in her back. "I think that might have been the longest drive ever."

"No argument here." George shrugged the stiffness from his shoulders. "How do we...uh, hmm, okay. That's kind of creepy."

In front of them, the gates stuttered inward with a screech of old metal.

"Faulty motion sensor?" Raven guessed. "Or maybe someone inside saw us arrive."

"Someone lives here?"

"Possibly." Humor sparked, and it felt good. "Whether feathered or human remains to be seen."

"How many times have you visited this, uh...?" The question faded to a stare.

With a faint chill skating along her spine, Raven followed her companion's gaze to a human-size bird huddled in a leafy stand of trees to their left.

The chill immediately lowered to a tingle.

"It's a raven-shaped boulder." She breathed out her relief. "They're scattered all over the property. You get used to it."

The clouds overhead darkened—or something did. Raven felt the air around her stir. And barely had time to raise her head before a silent shadow fell over her from behind.

CONNOR O'BRIEN STOOD alone in the fourth-floor attic of Blume House. He had an excellent view of the ocean waves that crashed and foamed over the rugged sweep of coastline that comprised Raven's Ridge. Almost as good was the view past the neighboring woods that bled into a clearing where last night he'd counted close to forty tents. That number had more than doubled today. He hated to think what tomorrow would bring.

He'd been told that a small army of people, many of them self-proclaimed psychics, descended on the ridge every three years for a three-day celebration known as Ravenspell. Not surprisingly, several of the participants or seekers or whatever the locals called them, arrived days in advance of the actual event which stretched from September sixth to the ninth. Then again, a party was a party, after all.

This particular party involved Hezekiah Blume's man-into-bird transformation, coupled with a tragedy that had occurred at a later point in time. All Connor really knew was that some form of gruesome death resided at the core of both things.

Coffee mug in hand, he rested a shoulder against the window frame, sipped and stared, and tried not to let his mind wander. Life was what it was, what it had to be. And what it was, in this case, was better than the alternative he'd been given once hell had opened its fiery jaws and demanded a sacrificial soul.

He spotted the glint of a lens near one of the smaller tents. Easing back a step, he took another drink. He wore black out of habit and usually stuck to the shadows, but neither precaution rendered him invisible—as he'd discovered mere days after his arrival here.

The Cove should have been a temporary stop at best. A place to think and regroup, to plan for a nebulous future. But one wrong turn combined with a squeaky floorboard had changed all of that. For the better, he liked to think.

He heard a low creak behind him. The screech of

hinges and muttered curse that followed were familiar enough to elicit a smile. "Better than a doorbell, cousin."

The new arrival snorted. "Not if you're the one who has to make the climb. Why are you always up here when I come by?"

"Same reason you always come by when I'm up here. Your campers are multiplying."

"Like rabbits in heat."

"Rabbits are born in heat." The vague amusement dissolved as Connor ran his gaze over the gathering ground. "Do they know the rules?"

"Inasmuch as I can make them known to a collection of airheads with ravens' feathers for brains and very little in the way of actual lives. Beware, though, the curiosity level is bound to go up as the sun goes down."

"And the drugs and alcohol begin to flow."

"Not much either of us can do to stop that. I'd set old Rooney on them—he can almost pass for the walking dead—except being what and who these people are, he'd probably fascinate more than frighten them. We'll have to settle for locked doors, latched windows and, ha-ha, good manners."

Connor shrugged. "It's not that much of a deal. I can avoid a trespasser or two for however long it takes your festival of ravens to play out."

"Sad to say, it can play for a rather long time. There's the lead-up crowd as you see, followed by the more serious event goers. Then you have Ravenspell itself, the inevitable hangers-on, and just when you think you're clear, you trip over a bevy of stragglers who refuse to pack their crystals and leave until forced to do so by whatever town councilor feels like bothering."

"Sounds like my uncle Dan's wedding reception." Connor finished his coffee, let his eyes scan the woods and the section of iron fence that bisected them. Another glint, this one of white metal caught his eye. He crouched for a closer look. When the metal flashed again, he nodded forward. "Front gate's open."

"What?" Annoyed, his companion bent and squinted. "Crap, it is. Stupid piece of junk works like every other contraption in the place—that being when it chooses to. Did anyone come through?"

"Not yet, but there's a truck outside."

The man next to him snarled. "I hate Ravenspell." His expression darkened. "I'll get rid of them."

With pleasure, Connor suspected, and struggled with a feeling he recognized clearly as envy. For some things more than others and for one thing above all. But the act of ousting an intruder definitely ranked in the top five.

"Make sure you know who you're dealing with," he advised when the attic door screeched open. "It doesn't take much of a mistake to get burned."

"Said the kettle to the pot. I'll give you the full rundown after—"

The sentence was interrupted by a sound. A short, sharp blast that echoed and rippled and brought Connor's eyes into full, wary focus.

His companion bent again. "Where?"

"Near the gate."

"Not my day." A warning finger came up. "Do not follow me."

Still in his crouch, Connor scoured the area. The sun had vanished under an enormous purple-black cloud. The air inside and out had gone still. But the memory of the blast remained and repeated in his head—as it did every night and would for the remainder of his life.

The memory of a gun being fired.

It took Raven several heart-thumping minutes to convince herself—and George—that a raven swooping down on them did not constitute an attack.

"I thought it was going to land on our heads." George returned the gun he'd fired to the back of his jeans and batted his short brown hair. "I felt its wings on my face."

"You felt air." Climbing back into the truck, and still jittery herself, Raven reached for the key. The engine started—and immediately began to knock.

"Is that mechanical or bird related?" George peered through the side window. "I don't see anything."

"Pretty sure it's not a raven on the roof." She checked the dash for red lights. "I get human anatomy, but the anatomy of a truck, not so much." After tapping the instrument panel, she eased the vehicle into gear. "Let's get to the house, shut if off and hope it heals itself, because I seriously doubt Raven's Cove will have an auto mechanic up to the challenge of fixing it."

The truck coughed and clanked and slowly limped its way into the courtyard of Blume House. She maneuvered it around a massive stone fountain carved into the shape of a bird's nest, smiled at the pair of enormous black ravens that surged up from each side, and cut the engine.

When they reached the veranda, George planted his hands on a vertical beam and gave a shaky laugh. "I just made a discovery. I'm afraid of large birds. I mean, I knew growing up that I didn't want one for a pet, but I had no idea I was terrified of them." He offered Raven a sheepish smile. "Sorry. I'm acting like a ten-year-old girl."

She wiggled the key Rooney had sent her into the ancient lock. "When I was ten, my friends and I used to dare each other to go into Mrs. Grumbacher's weed-infested yard after dark and steal leaves from her hawthorn bush."

"Who was Mrs....?"

"Local witch." She grinned at him over her shoulder. "Or so we believed."

With a smile ghosting around his lips, he pushed off. "I stand cut down and corrected.... Do you want me to try?"

"Be my guest." Raven dropped the key in his palm.

While he went to work, she returned to the courtyard to size up the house. "Some of these windows look low enough to crawl through."

"Cop here," George reminded. When twisting failed, he resorted to jabbing and rattling.

Out of deference to the late-summer humidity, Raven lifted the hair from her neck and held it there while she wandered away. "I'll see what I can find," she called back.

She shouldn't have accepted his offer of help. She'd realized that before she'd done it. So why had she done it? Because George had known and occasionally worked with Aidan? Probably, partly. Because she hadn't wanted to come here alone? Maybe. Because there was no danger of her being attracted to him?

Well, ouch, she thought, wincing as the question tightened the guilty strings in her midsection. When a more disturbing sensation joined them, however, she pushed the guilt aside, released her hair and turned in a circle as she walked.

What was it she'd been feeling for the past twelve plus months? Creeped out was a given, and annoyance came and went, depending on the circumstances and her mood. She didn't believe in ghosts. Not really. Her mother did, but that was a different thing.

The sensation dissipated when her gaze landed on a slightly elevated window. Which must mean she didn't feel immediately threatened. "Hope that's a good sign," she said, and, after checking the ground, waded into the tangle of weeds and wild bushes under the sill.

It surprised her that the pane slid up without much effort. She hoisted her butt onto the ledge, reminded herself that she was family and, bending under the glass, hopped onto the tiled floor.

She worked her way through boxes and broken shelves to a wide plank door. The latch turned with a gritty rasp that matched the sound of the hinges.

Old dust and the memory of dried herbs scented the air in a second, larger room that contained even bigger boxes and many more shelves. Something black and possibly feathered hung from a hook near the exit door. Not a bat, she hoped, or a dead raven, and kept an eye on the shadowy outline while she tugged on the iron ring. Thankfully, whatever it was remained motionless, allowing her to move quickly past.

Long and narrow, the third room was a hodgepodge of sinks, counters and cupboards. Beyond it was a corridor that led to a workroom filled with stacked chairs, a chipped blackboard and still more boxes.

She was passing under a light fixture the size of a compact car and listening to flies drone in the otherwise oppressive silence when she felt it again. The sensation of someone behind her, watching her, possibly close enough to touch her.

Swinging around, she searched the room. Although the windows were covered with curtains, there was enough light for her to be certain she was alone.

"Getting weird, Raven," she murmured. But wisdom had her turning another circle as she walked.

Still nothing and no one appeared.

Rocking her head from side to side, she located a third door and pulled it open. And was very nearly steamrollered by a man the size and shape of a sea lion. He slammed into her, reared back, then pushed her into the jamb and ran.

Raven's head struck wood. The room exploded briefly with stars. She stopped herself from falling over a wooden bench as feet thundered across the floor. Catching hold of the raised back, she regained her balance and, without a moment's hesitation, took off in the opposite direction.

She was halfway across a wide hall when another figure appeared. Like the first one, it plowed into her at a dead run. Or she plowed into it. Whatever the case, instead of shoving her aside, a pair of hands grasped her upper arms and held fast.

She glimpsed a red-eyed raven, sharp talons and an open beak as she was hauled kicking and clawing into a bared, male chest.

Chapter Three

She didn't scream—what would have been the point?—but instead recalled the self-defense maneuvers she'd learned as a child.

"Wait, don't…" the person holding her began, but she'd already planted her heel on his foot. When he swore, she fisted her hand and aimed for his throat.

He avoided the worst of the punch by feinting sideways—and uttering a growl just familiar enough that, instead of running, she scooped the hair from her face to stare in disbelief.

"Are you serious?" Fear warred with temper for control. "Steven?" Cousin Steven, the San Francisco lawyer? Here in Raven's Cove? Her shocked gaze skimmed the long hair, the assortment of pierced body parts and finally the exposed chest beneath an unstrung leather vest. "With a Hezekiah tattoo?"

He made a negating motion with his hand. "Don't talk, don't move, don't even breathe. Just stand there until I can think past the pain that's shooting like a damn pinball between my foot and my neck."

Raven complied, more out of astonishment than anything. But only until he straightened and started rubbing his throat. Then she swept her hair back all the way, straightened and arched her brows. "Okay, explain. First of all, what are you even doing on this coast? Second, what's the deal with that man—I think man—who came this close to giving me a concussion in his rush to get out?" When his eyes glinted, she stared him down. "Don't lie to me, Steven. I'm not nine years old anymore."

"A rather obvious statement, I'd say." Her cousin's glower faded to a scowl. "Any man you saw had no business being in this house, so we'll assume he was beating a hasty retreat. As for why I'm in the Cove, suffice to say that during the course of a certain sensitive trial, I took a wrong turn and got myself disbarred. Never having been concerned about rainy days, when the deluge hit the fan I ended up in very deep water. I was licking my wounds in an Oakland bar one night when old Rooney called me with a proposition. God knows how the news reached him, but it did, and his response was to point out that, as he was fast approaching the century mark, it might be prudent for him to turn the handling of his business affairs over to someone he could trust... Make a sarcastic comment about that last part, Raven, and I'll let it be known to every nut ball at Ravenspell that, Rooney notwithstanding, you're the most direct Hezekiah descendent currently in the Cove."

Raven couldn't stem her amusement. "So I guess, *How's it going?* would be a redundant question at this point."

"Ravenspell," he reminded. "Chock-full of loons."

"Yes, I've heard about it, and them."

Steven wiggled his jaw back and forth. "You've heard, but you've never come. Why is that—Raven?"

The amusement blossomed into a laugh. "Nice try, but you can't goad me anymore. I didn't come because my mother told me what life in the Cove was like for her. Being a direct descendent and a free thinker somehow combined to make her the most likely candidate to be possessed by Hezekiah's tortured spirit. Everything she did was scrutinized, analyzed and judged. She told me that 'spacey' was the kindest of the labels she was given."

"Yes, we all have our labels to bear."

Sensing a no-go zone, she switched tacks. "Where's Addie these days?"

His expression soured even further. "My sweet baby sister is as busy as the proverbial bee in San Francisco. On top of the clients she already had, she inherited most of mine. Don't you two keep in touch?"

"We Facebook, email and Twitter like the rest of the world, but not about work-related stuff. Maybe it was Addie who contacted Grandpa on your behalf."

"Why would she do that?"

Raven widened her eyes. "Because she loves you and probably wanted to help."

A creak of wood drew her gaze to the staircase. But only until the door behind her burst open and George stumbled in.

He halted to stare. "You're here."

"I found a window."

Beams of dusty sunlight bounced off a hanging mirror. George glanced over and blinked. "I, uh…" Trailing away, he cleared his throat, gave his glasses a poke and offered Steven a solemn nod.

Her cousin snorted. "Friend of yours?"

For a second, Raven thought she spied a movement on the stairs. Part of an arm or a shoulder. Whatever it was, it vanished too quickly for her to be sure. When Steven prodded her, she zoned back in. "Sorry, what did you ask? Oh, right, George. We drove up from Portland together with Grandpa's new kitchen appliances. I think the truck died in the courtyard."

Steven cupped her elbow. "In that case, what say we move this party to old Rooney's house. If your truck's dead, I'll hitch it to my four-by-four for a tow. You can brew a pot of tea, Rooney'll spike it, and while he's telling you about your mother's childhood escapades, George and I can unload his new purchases."

Nodding absently, Raven contemplated the wide staircase. And for the life of her couldn't figure out why her brain felt numb while her heart raced out of control in her chest.

IF HE'D BEEN THINKING, if he'd been able to think, Connor would have heard the footsteps long before the person making them turned the second-floor corner. As it was, a man the size of a walrus stopped dead and gaped at him as if he were Hezekiah Blume come to life.

Connor was tall, but this man topped six-seven and had to weigh close to three hundred pounds. So the fact that he held up two flipper-size palms and flinched astonished as much as it amused.

"I was looking for a bathroom." The flippers wagged. "Swear to God, I wasn't going to pilfer anything. My ma, she's into the woo-woo stuff. She and me, we live in Bangor. She wanted to come for the Ravenspell while she still could. But, hey, the woman's seventy-nine. Tough as flaming nails, but still—seventy-nine. I couldn't let her go off tenting alone. Man alive, though, those porta-johns are bad. So I came looking for something that wasn't like walking into a septic tank." He wiggled his upraised fingers. "D'you, uh, live here, then?"

The shadows that crisscrossed the corridor created a number of deep black pools. Connor knew by the way the man peered at him that he was standing in one of them.

"No one lives here," he said. Which was true and not

true. "Doesn't mean the place isn't privately owned or that the people who own it want strangers wandering up and down the halls."

Chastised, the man scuffed a heel across the carpet. "I'll say I'm sorry again, to you and the lady, too, if I see her."

Connor kept his tone casual. "Might be best all around if you put the whole wrongful entry thing out of your mind."

"Fine by me. Does the lady own the place?"

"Rooney Blume owns it. He's got twenty years on your mother and doesn't need to know about any of this."

"Sure, good, I mean—I won't come inside again. Swear."

For no reason he could fathom—and because he wouldn't be here long after sunset anyway—Connor took pity on the man. "There's a sink and toilet in the shed behind what's left of the western wall. Hasn't got a lock. If you're careful about making the climb, you can use it."

"Ma, too?"

The picture that formed brought a smile. "Yeah, why not, her, too."

The man's shoulders heaved. "Thanks, Mr...."

"Blume," he lied. "Steven. Don't let me see you again. Lawyers tend to have bigger problems with uninvited guests than cops do."

The man rubbed his hands down the legs of his pants. "If you say so. I'll just..." Jerking his head, he backpedaled swiftly down the hall.

Connor waited until he heard the rear stairwell door open and close before he moved.

The guy was a curiosity, but whether harmless or not didn't matter as much as it probably should. Getting the hell out, now *that* mattered. Because if he didn't leave, he might screw up and do something incredibly dangerous.

Again.

HE TIPTOED THROUGH the big house, listening at doors, peeking around corners and making a minimum amount of noise. It was a tedious task that had him sweating and truly in need of a bathroom by the time he reached an exit.

Under a purplish black cloud, he picked his way through a minefield of rubble on the west side of the house. Once the worst of it was behind him, he sank onto a rock to mop the back of his neck. He waited five minutes, breathing deeply, before digging out his cell phone and dialing the required number. He didn't think it was a good sign that his call was answered on the first ring.

"What?"

Start with the obvious, he told himself, leave the best for last. "I'm in Raven's Cove." He looked up at the imposing—and many said haunted—house. "Sort of."

"Raven Blume?"

Fear and a touch of superstition dimpled the skin on his arms. "Believe me when I tell you, I wouldn't be here if she wasn't."

"Can you see her?"

"Not exactly, but I heard her talking to a tattooed man a while back. He took her to see her grandfather, some old-as-the-hills coot named Rooney. She won't be leaving town in a hurry. Even if she wanted to, she couldn't. Her truck's giving her trouble."

"What's wrong with it?"

"It's making a funny sound."

"Because of you, or on its own?"

The man flailed a hand. "Did I mention the tattooed

man? He's like everywhere I go, and he watches the gate like a hawk, or maybe I mean a raven. The other Raven—Blume—shut her truck off for less than three minutes and only walked a few yards away. There was no time to mess up the engine. Which I wouldn't have done anyway because she has a trigger-happy nerd riding shotgun with her."

"If I ask who the nerd is will you answer in one sentence or less?"

"I don't know who he is."

"Not exactly the response I'd hoped for."

A shiver crawled up the big man's spine. "Look, you wanted me to do a job, and I'm doing it. You said follow her to Maine, and I did."

"I also told you under no circumstances to lose her."

A hint of ornery snuck through. "I didn't come all this way to sleep in a frigging tent and listen to crazy people talk about a raven man. I'm on her. I've also got news you might want to hear, and it's not something you paid me to find out."

"I'm all ears and anticipation."

Giving his overheated neck another wipe, the man glanced back at the house. "I bumped into someone when I was heading out to call you just now. And I hope you're sitting down, 'cause your world's gonna rock clear to China when I tell you who I think it was."

SHE MANAGED TO ESCAPE. Unfortunately, it took the better part of two hours to do it, because Rooney, being Rooney, wanted to talk. About many things, but mostly, Raven discovered, about the infamous history of Blume House.

Because she already knew the legend of Hezekiah's transformation, he had sidetracked to a secondary story that also played into Ravenspell.

"As a doctor," he began with a mostly toothless smile, "you'll appreciate that Blume House was used as a facility for convalescing soldiers when the Great War ended in 1918. That was many years after Hezekiah's time, but evil is notorious for its patience, to say nothing of its staying power." He filled his black mug with a one-to-three blend of tea and whiskey. "It's said that some of what infected Hezekiah managed to escape the transformation." His blue eyes sharpened on her face. "Can you guess where it might have gone, Granddaughter?"

"I'd like to think hell, but being a Blume, I'll say into the fabric of the house?"

Rooney beamed at her. "You're a Blume, through and through, young Raven. Which is why you won't be afraid that such a dreadful thing as happened in September of 1919 will happen when that same portion of Blume House becomes a medical facility once more."

Amused, she regarded him across the table. "I'll bite, Grandpa. What dreadful thing happened back in 1919?"

"When all was said and done, two men wound up dead. One was murdered, the other killed himself."

"Why would two deaths—never mind. Go on."

"The killer believed that the man he murdered had caused his twin brother to die on the battlefield a month or so before the war ended. It was an eye for an eye, he claimed, but not in a way that satisfied."

"That way being...?"

"You can't guess?"

Raven watched Steven, George and a pair of neighbors who'd volunteered to help, wrestle the old range through Rooney's barely wide enough cottage door, before sliding her gaze back to the old man. "I'll speculate that either the killer wanted his victim to die slowly and in pain but couldn't pull that off with medical staff and other convalescing soldiers around, or he'd have preferred to kill the victim's brother instead of him, making it a true eye for an eye."

"Number two's the bingo," Rooney congratulated. "Problem was, the man who died had no kin. Made the choice of victims a moot point."

Raven masked her teasing tone. "And this story relates to the evil that secreted itself in the walls of Blume House, how?" Then replied at the same time as her great grandfather, "You can't guess?"

The old man cackled. "I'm gonna enjoy having you nearby, I think. Fresh blood's what you are and what this town's been needing for a long time now."

"I'm truly hoping the evil doesn't see it that way." She lifted her cup but knew better than to take a sip. "As for my guess, I'll postulate that the murderer wasn't a man who enjoyed killing—thus the need to convalesce after the war—nor had he previously been the kind of person who would commit an act of vengeance regardless of the crime. Therefore, the evil in Blume House must have infected him and forced him to commit an act so abhorrent that his mind shattered. Which relegates his story—by virtue of the evil takeover and its September date—to the lore that is Ravenspell."

"Impeccable logic, Granddaughter." Rooney toasted her and drank heartily. "Of course, time has a way of changing things, and it's now generally believed that the evil has spread beyond the walls of the house to the Blume-owned grounds surrounding it."

"Well, I guess you couldn't expect it to sit around waiting for its next victim to walk through the front door."

Rooney gave another delighted cackle. He also took another drink. "I do believe when my time on earth is done, I'll pass the Raven's Tale torch and all that goes with it on to you...."

Someone dropped a heavy object outside, and Steven started to swear. Grateful for the reprieve, Raven helped Rooney to his feet, watched him deal with her cousin's temper, then slipped back into his cottage for the keys to the Jeep he'd told her she could use.

That the vehicle possessed a valid license plate didn't surprise her. That Rooney possessed a license to drive it shocked her speechless. But only until she heard the warning rumbles of thunder over the water. Then her focus shifted.

The road to Blume House split the woods in several places. It allowed for glimpses of the high ridge in several more. Close to the top, dense trees gave way to an odd-shaped clearing. The Ravenspell campsite, according to Steven, whose opinion of its current occupants, had been reflected in the curl of his lip.

On this, Raven's third drive by, the site seemed more active than before as people with beads, braids and bandannas staked waterproof tarps over their tents. The big purple cloud had given way to a roiling black mass that extended from Blume House to the town center. There was no wildlife to be seen, and the only birdsong Raven heard when she pulled Rooney's Jeep into the parking bay Steven had pointed out earlier belonged to the woodland ravens.

Weird, she decided, then upped the description to creepy as she regarded the house from a new perspective. The facade didn't quite scream evil, but it had a forbidding look about it, as if it were expecting something less than wholesome to unfold.

Probably not the best thought she could have, Raven

reflected, given that her nerves were still in overdrive from her first foray inside.

She tugged a short jacket over her tank top, glanced at the cobblestone path ahead of her and wished she'd taken the time to change out of her wedge sandals and into something more practical.

Blume House possessed multiple entranceways, but Rooney had promised that one key worked all of them. And not to worry, he wouldn't tell Steven she'd gone back there alone. Evidently, her cousin had grown very proprietary about the place. However, as the property was no more Steven's than hers, and the actual deed was in her great-grandfather's name, Raven figured she could handle any objections he might make.

Not so easy to handle was the feeling that washed over her when she nudged the side door open and squeezed inside.

Whatever its source, the ripple of energy that electrified her skin lingered for several seconds. She acknowledged it, then did her best to make it disappear.

The last of the day's sunlight stole through slender breaks in the cloud mass. Bumping the door closed with her hip, Raven waited for her eyes to adjust.

The bowling alley room must have been an arboretum at one time. Pots and planters stood like soldiers on the tiled floor. Baskets filled with stringy dead plants hung before a wall of dirty windows. There were wicker chairs covered with sheets and two large tables were piled one on top of the other.

Pushing off, she rubbed at the gooseflesh that refused to leave her arms. Whatever she'd experienced in the great hall was making a strong and stubborn return visit. Oddly enough, she didn't think this current feeling was connected to the one she'd experienced so often in the past. There was no sense of being followed or watched here. It was more, she thought, like a prickle of anticipation.

The timeworn joists groaned. Beyond the walls, ocean waves tumbled over rock to crash against the craggy base of the cliff. Raven acknowledged the probability of a wild night ahead, and tried to ignore the fresh chill that made her shiver.

With no clear sense of why she'd returned, she left the arboretum in search of the main entry hall. She was making her way along a corridor cloaked in shadows when she detected a sound on the floor above.

It wasn't a settling creak, and it had nothing to do with the approaching storm. This sound had a measured quality to it, the stealthy, repetitive protest of hardwood under someone's slow-moving feet.

Whoever it was was walking from Raven's left to her right. Toward the main stairwell?

As her eyes scanned the ceiling, a door screeched open. Seconds later, the stair treads groaned.

Keeping her eyes on the beams, she pulled out her iPhone and set her thumb on speed dial. If Rooney answered, Steven would come. He'd curse her from here to Rochester, but he'd come.

Or she could call George. But—well, no.

Twenty-one creaks later, the stairs fell silent. The shriek of hinges that followed was probably a door opening.

Or a coffin.

Sliding her thumb back and forth over the speed dial button, Raven watched the shadows. And felt her heart leap into her throat when the floor behind her gave a protracted squeak.

Okay. Damn, but okay.

She ducked into a banquet-size dining room. Still a Blume, she reminded herself. Right was on her side.

Unless Wrong was packing a gun, in which case, she was in serious trouble. "Calling Steven," she said while she jogged across the room.

She hit Rooney's number. However, before the dialing process ended, the gates of hell sprang open.

Doors slammed, one, two, three. Someone grunted. She counted a series of thuds, heard a scuffle in progress and veered away from it.

Furniture scraped and fell. The racket came from everywhere, or seemed to. She couldn't separate one sound from another. Were there three people here besides her? Four?

Through a blur of mounting terror, Raven struggled to calculate where the nearest escape might be. It didn't ease her mind that the thunder had grown louder or that she was picking up new and closer sounds.

Gusts of wind beat angry fists against the outer walls—wherever they were. A loud crack preceded the sound of breaking glass. On the heels of that, all the lights she'd switched on as she moved through the house died.

Pressing her back to a tall cabinet, she listened to Rooney's phone ring. And ring and ring and ring.

"Come on, Grandpa," she pleaded. "Pick up."

But he didn't, and neither did his voice mail.

She was scrolling for George's number when someone barreled into the room. He shot past her at a dead run, but thankfully didn't stop.

Far ahead, Raven spied a dusty sliver of light trickling in through a high window. As the gloom dissipated, a door took shape.

Dropping her iPhone back in her bag, she arranged the strap crosswise from shoulder to hip. Behind her, a stream of staccato thumps erupted. There was another crash and finally a shout.

Way too close, she decided, and ran for the door.

"Open," she muttered when the latch stuck. "Damn you, turn and open."

She shook the handle, twisted it, even used her hip and shoulder on the heavy panels. The latch clicked but the door itself refused to give.

She cursed it under her breath, then snapped her head to the left as someone's feet landed on the floor close by. Whoever it was stood and headed straight for her.

With one panicked push, Raven got the stuck hinges to release.

She felt damp air blast her face and started to dart across the threshold.

But, suddenly, there was no floor beneath her. She was flying sideways with a pair of arms locked tight around her.

She steeled herself for a hard landing. That it didn't materialize would have puzzled her if fear hadn't been screaming at her to break the tackle.

She squirmed and fought and got in a single hard punch to her captor's face. Certain it was a man, she wrenched her body sideways and freed a knee.

Whether it connected directly with his groin or not wasn't clear, but he swore so it must have come close.

"Hold still," he said in a low growl. "Raven, stop fighting me."

He held her wrists, but it was his voice more than his action that stilled her.

His hair brushed her cheeks, and she could almost make out the details of his features in the light that filtered through the high window. She added in the scent of his skin—frighteningly familiar—the shape of his muscles, the feel of his body against hers, and...

Already racing, her heart knocked into her ribs. She couldn't speak or move, was half-afraid to breathe as she stared into his eyes.

Black eyes. Black hair.

Black Irish…

The grip on her wrists loosened, tripping an alarm in her head. It was a trick, it had to be. A bad joke, or worse, a hallucination. She fought him again, then because it was the only weapon left when his fingers tightened, attempted to bite his arm.

"Raven…"

"Let me go!" Working a foot free, she lashed out at his ankle. "You're not—"

He cut her off with his mouth. Just trapped her lips and shocked every thought, every objection, every shred of sanity she possessed into silence. This time when he loosened his grip, it was to raise her arms over her head and dive in even deeper.

Raven's numbed senses slithered into a boneless abyss where reality and fantasy met and misted, and the impossible simply floated away.

Until his mouth left hers, and her mind jolted back to life.

Planting her palms on his chest, she shoved him back far enough that she could scramble to her hands and knees. Heart slamming, she confronted his shadowed silhouette.

"You're a lie," she accused. "You're not here. You can't be—" the denial turned to dust in her throat "—here."

Maybe logic said he couldn't be here, but he very much was. He'd kissed her, so she knew it was true. As astonishment faded, all that remained was the echo of a name that curled through her head like a wisp of ghost-gray smoke.

Aidan…

Chapter Four

"I'm losing my mind." Sitting back on her heels, Raven drilled her index finger into her temples. He'd vanish any second now. Like the ghost he had to be. Then she'd know she'd gone insane.

Narrowing her eyes to slits, she stared at the gorgeous, achingly familiar and still-shadowed face of the man she loved. The dead man she'd continued to love for the past two years, three weeks and one day.

At length, the keen edge of temper sliced through the fog still muddling her brain. "You were killed in an explosion. You went into an abandoned theater, and you didn't come out. I saw your body. I…" Stopping there, she worked backward through the nightmare. "I didn't see your body. No one did. All we had was Captain Beckett's word that you'd died."

She wanted to pull away when he hauled her to her feet. "We can't stay here."

Someone's body collided with a nearby wall. A snarl and several thuds reached them.

"We need to go," he repeated. "Now."

"What? No. Why? Never mind." Tugging free, she backed toward the open door. "I still think I'm hallucinating."

But this time she didn't push him when he caught her

wrist and set his lips next to her ear. "Whatever you think, we can't get out that way."

"Yes, we can. I felt the wind when the latch gave."

"Wind won't support you, and solid ground's ten feet down. That door opens to the west wing, the one Hurricane Enid tore apart."

Before she could respond, a human mass splatted on the floor in front of them. Her eyes went wide. "Steven?"

For the second time that day, her cousin jabbed an accusing finger at her. "I swear to God, you've been trouble since you were born. You just had to come back here, didn't you?" He crawled to his feet, dusted off. "What the hell's going on?"

"No idea." Aidan—God, really? Really?—nodded forward. "There's an exit on the south wall that borders the woods. We need to get to it."

Steven scowled. "I got one guy to take off, but there's another here somewhere."

"I tackled him into a wall," Aidan said. "Don't think it slowed him down much."

Okay, maybe she wasn't insane, Raven conceded, but the situation definitely was.

Her cousin glanced into the shadows. "Someone's coming."

Bulls made grunting sounds like that, Raven thought through a haze. Too bad it wasn't a bull thundering across the room toward them.

Aidan shoved her ahead and brought up the rear while Steven led the way toward a barely visible access hall next to a boarded-up stairwell.

She'd felt this way in her nightmares, many times. Off balance, terrified and out of step, both with herself and with the circumstances that spun like a mad kaleidoscope around her. Was it possible, she wondered, for the lunatic gene to be passed down through blood?

"Turn left," Aidan directed from behind. "One more corridor and we'll be in the butler's pantry."

Or in deeper trouble than before if the hallway dead-ended, because she could hear the footsteps pounding along in pursuit.

Thankfully, the corridor did open to a pantry. Steven pointed sideways. "Decoy," he said, and vanished with noisy intent into the dark.

Aidan grabbed Raven's hand. "Come on."

She didn't object, merely glanced back once, then ran with him through the door.

Outside, the cliff rocks loomed large and menacing. The wind swirled in fitful circles, picking up and spitting out leaves at random.

When she started to skirt the house, Aidan caught her arm and gestured at the woods. "Do you know where the Ravenspell campsite is?"

"Yes." Her breath came in spasms now, and not entirely from fear.

"Get to the site and stay there. I need to know who's after us."

Even through the gloom and the hair that kept flying in her face, Raven saw his expression. She'd called it his cop look and found it amusing way back when. Now she wanted to punch him.

Or kiss him.

He decided the matter by yanking her forward for a kiss that made her go hot and tingly from the top of her head to the tips of her toes.

One, two, three seconds' worth of delicious, soul-stirring kiss. Yet even as her mind and body reeled, he repeated, "Campsite," spun her toward it and vanished.

"Well, Jesus." Raven took a precious moment to finger her lips in disbelief before common sense kicked in and she ran. Along the dirt path, into the woods and down the trail to the clearing.

Only Aidan would know she'd find it. Only he would understand that she had an internal GPS better than most tracking dogs. He would also know that, although panic wasn't a foreign concept to her, she possessed the ability to think and act her way through it. Or she did until a single gunshot brought her to a halt on the wooded trail.

The sound echoed and pulsed and strangled the breath in her lungs as she swung to face it.

That single resounding shot had come from Blume House.

AIDAN HEARD THE SHOT and pulled his own gun from the waistband of his jeans. *Goodbye Connor, hello trouble.*

A dozen deadly possibilities whizzed through his head, but in spite of them, he had to believe that Raven would reach the clearing safely. It was imperative that he discover who'd invaded Blume House, how many were there, and why they'd gone inside.

His instincts were rusty. He accepted that. But his resolve to protect Raven hadn't changed. Nothing and no one was going to hurt her.

He crouched for a moment in the rubble of the ruined west wing. Wind whistled around chunks of what had once been a large addition to Blume House. Already, the early-evening light had vanished. With the exception of two emergency floods in the courtyard, darkness, broken only by the daunting silhouette of the house, ruled.

Holding his position, Aidan watched the perimeter and listened for anything out of the ordinary. The barely discernible crunch of rock and plaster to his right qualified. Planting a knee, he pivoted toward it.

Both the crunch and the person who'd made it froze. Luckily, so did Aidan's trigger finger.

Raven's eyes flicked from the tip of his gun to his shadowed face. "I heard a shot."

A flood of emotion too deep and raw to separate rushed through him. Reaching forward, he brought her to the ground.

He started to point out that this was not the Ravenspell campsite, then thought to hell with it and set his mouth on hers.

He wanted to devour her, to lose himself and the nightmare of his current life in her. For one suspended moment, nothing mattered more than touching her, tasting her, feeling the curves of her body beneath his roaming hands.

He was hungry for her. Hell, he was ravenous. Two years was too damn long for his self-control not to crack and give his sorely deprived senses what they'd been craving since his "death." Far back in his mind, those same senses reminded him that every second of that deprivation had been worthwhile.

With a sound caught between disbelief and desperation, Raven twined her fingers in his hair and locked his mouth on hers.

He understood the feeling, if not consciously—because his mind and body were too lost in her to think with any degree of clarity—then on an instinctive level. He tumbled from feeling to feeling to feeling, only to land in a place where rational thought no longer existed. He wanted more, and all he cared about was getting it.

Even so, he let her pull just far enough away to ask, "Why did you lie to me, Aidan? Why to me?"

The bad light might hide the expression in her mist-green eyes, but not the tone of her question. He recognized hurt over a jagged layer of anger. She could love him, be crazy happy to find him alive, kiss him senseless and still want to kick his ass from here to California.

"You know the answer, Raven," he replied with care. "In a name, it's Johnny Demars."

"Because he thought he'd killed you in the...ahh."

That single syllable said it all.

"Demars didn't set those explosives, you did. You figured if I believed you were gone, he'd believe it, too." She leaned back in, let her lips curve against his. "How very clever of you, Lieutenant McInnis. You and Captain Beckett."

He deflected the fist she would have plowed into his stomach, but missed the hand that took aim at his right cheek and jaw.

Shoving back and away, she added heat to the sting with a daggerlike glare.

"Two years, Aidan. I've lived in hell for two years so Johnny Demars would buy your death. This was Beckett's idea, wasn't it? Together you'd outsmart that smart-ass crime lord." With a humorless laugh, she raised her eyes to the night sky. "My God, did either of you give even a passing thought to the prospect of setting up and arresting the man for attempted murder? Of course not. Better you should pretend to die and spend the rest of your life living like a rat on the coast of Maine." Thoroughly irritated now, she stood. "We could have died together, Aidan. Here, in Mongolia, at the North Pole—I wouldn't have cared where. All you had to do was... What?"

He dragged her roughly down beside him, no doubt doubling her annoyance. "Someone's creeping along the back of the house."

"Where?" Instantly sidetracked, she followed his gaze through the of hurricane wreckage to a wall bordered by clumps of weeds and bushes. "I don't see... Wait, yes I do." She squinted into the darkness. "From the bulk and shape of him, that could be the guy I ran into earlier. Or he ran into me. I thought of a sea lion back then, but now I'm thinking creepy crawler."

"I'm thinking he has no business being here."

"Do you want to tell him that or should I?"

"I'll do it." Aidan drew the gun he'd stuffed back into his waistband. "In a roundabout way, we've met."

"Have you?" Her silvery tone made it clear he'd said the worst possible thing. "So Captain Beckett, our creepy crawler and Steven, aka, Benedict Arnold, all knew you were in the Cove. How—cozy."

"I don't love your cousin, Raven."

"Neither do I anymore."

Mild amusement sparked. "I'd say Steven was in deep trouble, if I wasn't in more of it myself." He kept his eyes on the tiptoeing man. "He's moving away from the shed."

"Creepy lives in a shed?"

"No, and odds are he's not living in a tent, either."

"Meaning he presented himself to you as a camper?"

"Here for Ravenspell with his seventy-nine-year-old mother." Aidan felt the exasperated look she cast him. "Yeah, I get it."

"I'll say it anyway, for emphasis. You need to hope, seriously hope, that your new friend's mother doesn't bear a resemblance to one of Johnny Demars's hired killers."

"Hope's my middle name these days." Angling his gun skyward, Aidan turned to her. "Whatever happens, I want you to promise me you won't do—"

"Anything stupid?" She moved a finger between them. "We have met, right?"

"I've got enough to regret already, Raven." Taking her chin in his hand, he tipped her head up for a brief but fiercely protective kiss. "I don't want you hurt."

"Way too late for that, I'm afraid. However, in an effort to keep us both alive, I promise to let you deal with— uh…" Dipping slightly, she regarded the house. "I think something spooked him."

Aidan looked over and swore. Instead of tiptoeing, the man was starting to run. Awkwardly, but he was moving much faster now than before.

"Okay, that's it," he muttered. "Stay here, this time, Raven." And with a quick left to right look, he took off.

It surprised him when two shots went off inside the house. They didn't slow him down since neither one had been fired anywhere near Raven, but they proved the danger factor was escalating rapidly.

First things first, he decided. When his quarry stumbled, he tucked his gun away and went for the tackle.

Misstep notwithstanding, taking the man out was like trying to bring down a linebacker barehanded. The man staggered a little, but would have broken Aidan's grip easily if his foot hadn't landed in a rut and sent him crashing into a wall.

Rolling clear, Aidan came up on his knees with his gun drawn.

"Don't shoot." Frantic hands waved him off. "I don't want anyone getting hurt, most of all me."

Aidan tasted blood from a cut at the corner of his mouth. "Talk to me, pal. And not about bathrooms. What are you doing here, and who pulled the trigger inside?"

"I don't know. I swear to God, I don't. I really did come here to use that outside bathroom." When Aidan raised his gun, the flapping became more agitated. "I'm not lying. All I have on me is a Swiss Army knife."

"What about your mother?"

"Oh, well, that's different. Her father was in the war. He left her a nasty-looking revolver. She keeps it in her, um, you don't really care, do you?"

"What's your name?"

The man waggled his fingers. "Smith. Fergus Smith."

"Why were you skulking along the back wall of the house?"

"Well, I heard shots being fired, didn't I? Sure, when I first got here, I wanted to know why the shotgun guy from this afternoon was jimmying a window and crawling inside, but I wasn't about to take a bullet for wondering."

"Who's the shotgun guy?"

"The guy who was riding shotgun in the white truck with the pretty lady. For all I know, he's the one doing the shooting. He tried to off a raven earlier today."

"You saw that happen, huh?"

Smith squirmed in discomfort. "From an upstairs window, while I was—you know."

"Looking for a bathroom. Did you see anyone else?" Aidan asked. "Tonight? After you followed the shotgun guy into Blume House?"

Smith made a flailing gesture. "Man, I don't know what I saw. Shadows moving, people running—me being one of them. I just wanted out… What was that?" he demanded. "Did you hear something?"

Calculating that she'd given it two full minutes before coming after him, Aidan rolled his tight neck muscles. "Your rear approach needs work, Raven."

"So does your peripheral hearing." She hopped down next to him, tapped his arm and pointed. "We've got company."

Which he actually had detected, but having recognized

her cousin's disgruntled tread, hadn't been concerned enough to address.

Steven grumbled his way into sight. "Easy job, no stress. Two, maybe three years, and I'd be ready to jump back into the shark tank." He raised his voice. "You listen to a damn thing Rooney says, Raven, and you'll wind up loonier six months on than you were when you got to this crazy bird town. I caught someone, Aidan—for about thirty seconds. Got kicked in the crotch, almost lost the use of my right arm, and if my nose isn't broken, it's only because, when I foolishly attempted to teach my nine-year-old sister and Raven to kickbox, I was forced to learn the fine art of ducking fast."

Aidan scanned the surrounding area. "Was it George?"

Raven brought her head around. "You think George was inside Blume House?"

"Fergus here saw him climb through one of the windows."

"And you trust Fergus here to be telling the truth? No offense," she added with a glance at the big man.

"None taken. But I did see him. The guy riding with you in the white truck went into the house through a window."

"Call it another link in an increasingly bizarre chain of events," Aidan suggested, "and try not to dwell on it."

"As a non-cop, I'll do my best." She turned to her cousin. "Are you sure it was George?"

"Hell no. Fergus here saw him, not me. I was shadowboxing." Reaching into his vest pocket, Steven pulled out a cell phone and tossed it to Aidan. "He dropped this. It'll probably fill in the name gap."

Tucking away his gun, Aidan took the device and immediately looked at Raven.

"What?"

He indicated himself, then her. "Techno-spaz, super-geek."

She shot him a smile that didn't bode well for their future alone time. But she held out her palm. "Okay, give it."

He watched her play for a moment before a flicker of lightning diverted him. He'd seen the same thing earlier in the vicinity of the Ravenspell campsite. "We need to get into the house."

"No way." Fergus Smith was adamant. "That place is spooked. Lights on, lights off, everything creaking and groaning and wailing. How do we know there aren't ghosts in the walls?"

"We don't." Aidan tracked a strange gust of wind as the sky lit up yet again. "But believe me when I tell you, there are worse things in this world than a ghost or two.... Something?" he asked Raven, who was pondering the on-screen display.

"Not sure." She scrolled forward, then back. "It is George's phone. It looks like he made a call while I was talking to Grandpa in the cottage. There's no name or number, but someone called him back a few minutes later."

"What's the name on the incoming?"

"All it says is Gort. Outgoing was placed at 5:53 p.m. Reply, I assume, came at 5:56." She looked up into his shielded eyes and narrowed her own. "That is not a happy expression, Aidan. Who's Gort?"

His gaze shifted to Blume House. "Police tag for Demars is Spaceman, but George thought Gort was a better fit. Deadly robot, no face."

"Like in that black-and-white movie where all the machines stopped working." Fergus Smith gave a sheepish shrug. "My ma watches old space movies."

"So does George." Raven paged sideways. "The communication from Gort lasted four and a half minutes. Shortly after that, George returned to Blume House— not sure how—and climbed through a window. I wonder what or who he was hoping to find?"

The resentment in her voice was obvious, but under it was a strong sense of disappointment. In George and in him, but mostly, Aidan sensed, in herself for misjudging a trusted friend's character.

"It's done, Raven. There's no way back. Demars knows I'm alive and in the Cove."

Her eyes shot to his. "Then you have to leave. Now. Tonight."

Everything inside him hardened. "Not an option. Demars wants to finish this, and so do I. And it can't be finished on the run."

Exasperation replaced fear. "So you're going to take him on in Raven's Cove?" She walked away and straight back. "That's suicide, pure and simple. Demars will send the best he's got to kill you. Do you have any idea what the best he's got looks like?"

"No, but I know what George looks like, so I have a starting point."

"If George is smart, he'll have hitched a ride to Portland by now and be on a homebound plane by the time Demars's hit man shows up."

Aidan's eyes glinted in the next fork of lightning. "You're not factoring in Demars's mindset, Raven. George won't be going anywhere before that hit man shows. And it'll be a toss-up what happens when he does."

A false smile came and went from Steven's lips. "I knew I should have stayed in San Francisco, just knew it."

"And I shoulda used a porta-john," Smith mumbled.

Raven poked a finger into Aidan's stomach. "You can't fight Demars alone. You know that, or you should. At least let Beckett in on what's happening, where George is and what he's… Oh, God, what's that look about? What are you planning to do?"

"What you probably expect," he replied, and couldn't quite keep the gleam of anticipation out of his eyes. "What I should have done two years ago. I'm going to off his hit man, then hunt the faceless bastard down and end this nightmare once and for all."

As he spoke, the wind whipped up and over the walls of Blume House. And for a single freakish moment, Aidan thought it resembled a man's mad laughter.

IT WAS DONE. FOR BETTER or worse—and his stomach strongly suggested worse—he'd placed the call and gotten the expected response.

Alone, on the side of the road that led to Raven's Cove, he waited. Three hours, Demars had told him in a computer-altered voice that made George's blood run cold. Someone would be there in three short hours.

A clap of thunder sent fresh chill blades down his spine. He stood in the wind, nervous fingers snapping, his glasses askew, with tears streaming over his cheeks. He knew why he'd done it, he just didn't know why he hadn't thought it through better first.

When the thunder came again, he squeezed his eyes closed. But he couldn't block the sound of Demars's distorted voice.

"Keep her there!"

"Keep Raven here?" George had repeated, baffled. "What does she have to do with any of this?"

The reply had been swift, the distortion a shrill and horrible sound.

Keep her there!

More tears spilled. What if Demars sent the big guy?

Killing was a thing he did for money. Torment and torture were his ultimate goals. And women, particularly beautiful women like Raven, provided him with the most enjoyment.

Or worse, maybe he'd send Weasel, the one with the knife. Weasel liked to cut people up, and attractive women were his favorite kind of people. Turning his face skyward, George breathed out in rapid whooshes. Until a pair of headlights cut through the gloom and he stopped breathing altogether.

The big guy drove a four-by-four, didn't he? But Weasel might, too. Either way, the truck with the smoke-black windows and superbright headlights had pulled to a stop five feet in front of him.

Demars's words echoed in his head. *Keep her there!* And now, here was one of his twisted hit men, come to Raven's Cove to take out the man who'd killed his son.

An eye for an eye, George thought as the driver of the four-by-four waited for him to approach. He'd heard the expression recently but couldn't remember where. Didn't care.

He didn't lift his head until the window opened—and a gleaming 9 mm semiautomatic gun came out to greet him.

Chapter Five

"My mother was right about Raven's Cove." Feeling a little as if she'd been hit with a stun gun, Raven looked over her shoulder at the fog that had begun to slither in from the ocean. "You come for a visit and bam, five minutes later, the town jumps into a rabbit hole and takes you with it." When Aidan stopped moving, she bumped into his back. Rubbing her nose, she said, "I don't think this is the best place for us to talk."

"Alone in a crowd, angel." Keeping her firmly behind him, he pushed his way into a shabby seaside bar called Two Toes Joe's. "Unfortunately, this isn't your typical Tuesday night crowd."

"No?" She dodged a man with big feet and an even bigger drunk on. "Interesting that you'd know that."

"Being a ghost is thirsty work." He sent her a quick grin. "I've come here three times in two years, Raven, and never as myself."

"Meaning you have an alter ego here in the Cove."

"Your great-grandfather's sitting next to the dartboard."

She waved at a cloud of thick, mostly illegal smoke. "I saw him, and, large crowd notwithstanding, I guarantee he's seen us right back."

"No one's eyes are that good." When two fishermen

vacated a corner booth, Aidan nabbed it and waited while she slid onto the worn wooden bench.

The music was a raspy fiddle-hornpipe combo, the air a sticky, gray miasma, and unless she'd gone color-blind, the beer she'd just glimpsed had been green. Lovely.

Unconcerned, Aidan went with a mug of tap ale. Raven regarded a passing pitcher and opted for club soda. When a puffy-faced male server appeared to take their order, he stared so long and hard she brushed her cheek.

"Am I smudged or something?"

"Or something," Aidan agreed. But it was an absent reply. His eyes hadn't stopped moving since they'd entered.

She tracked them now to the bar. "Are we meeting someone?"

"No, just looking. I haven't been out much lately."

Resignation slipped in. "And here we go. Straight to the crux of a conversation I never in my wildest dreams expected to have. Except—oh, no, wait—I haven't actually had what you'd call dreams since Gaitor told me you'd been blown into a million unidentifiable—should have clued in right there—pieces. My life became a full-scale nightmare at that point, and the scary thing is, it doesn't feel done. In fact, I feel like I'm about to jump from a nightmare straight into a night terror."

He waited until the server deposited their drinks before turning his dark gaze on her. "How long are you planning to stay pissed at me?"

A glimmer of unlikely amusement blossomed into a laugh. "Well, duh." Propping her elbows, she moved a finger between them. "Two years' worth of mourning wasted, pal. And I'll tell you something you probably don't know. Every six months your grandmother calls me up and tells me I have to come to New York for an anniversary wake. I go, we cry, she makes sure I'm not seeing anyone, then she drags me to Mass and gets a priest to bless me just in case the evil Blume thing has any merit. Afterward, she makes me promise to phone her every Sunday at 9:00 p.m. sharp so she'll know I'm all right."

"Hey, you marry into an Irish family, you're in it for life."

"I thought that very thing when we said 'I do.' In for life, for better or worse, till death—as in the real deal—do us part."

"Us do part," he corrected, and caused her temper to spike.

"You had no right to do what you did to me, Aidan. I knew before I married you that nothing about being a cop's wife would be easy. I also knew before you decided to pull a Houdini that Johnny Demars was vindictive as hell."

"Not vindictive, Raven, vicious. There's a difference."

"You wind up dead either way."

"Except in the second scenario, you beg for it. And begging is merely a prelude to his idea of fun and games."

She spotted a dusty, red-eyed raven tangled in the old fishing net that hung on the wall beside him. "I can't believe you faked your own death, put me and your family through hell and spent two years—with the prospect of countless more—living like a phantom in Raven's Cove, all because you were too afraid of what Johnny Demars might do to you to face it like the cop I know you are."

"The cop you thought I was. Same verb, different tense. Some people can and often do disappoint their loved ones. I can't change what I did any more than George can take back the call we both know he made.

We make our choices and whatever the fallout might be, that's what we're left to face. Forced to face, in my case and in yours."

The faintest trace of Irish left over from his early childhood slipped through as he leaned in on his forearms to make his point. He wanted her to believe him, desperately wanted it. But she couldn't.

Bubbles rose and burst in her cloudy glass. Watching them, she said, "The guy who served us just now has a goiter. It's making his neck swell. His voice could be hoarse from all the smoke in here, but I doubt it. His face is puffy, and his skin looks dry. I saw him for less than thirty seconds, Aidan, and I'd stake my medical reputation on the fact that he's hypothyroid."

Aidan's dark brows came together. "That's not fatal, is it?"

"Only if there's a tumor involved, which in most cases, there isn't. Point is, the server needs medical treatment, and you need a big reality check if you think I'm going to believe, even for a minute, that you're afraid of Johnny Demars."

Sitting back, he took a drink of the greenish beer. "I'd be a fool if I wasn't."

"You'd be a fool to underestimate him, but you've never been afraid of risking your life."

"If you believe that, maybe you don't know me as well as you think." He cast her a sideways look. "You want to make me into a superhero, and that's not what I am. I'm sorry if that disappoints you, but it's the truth. Johnny Demars scares the hell out of me. There's no walking away from a man like that. Screw with him, whether intentionally or not, and you're going to die. At some point, and in whatever manner he dictates—usually long and painful—you will die."

"But you'll go after him now," Raven countered. "Take out his hit man and set your sights on him now." The crowd noise swelled a little as the dim lights of the waterfront bar flickered. "What you're saying isn't you, Aidan. What I said before, that's you."

He rolled the unappealing contents of his mug. "I have no choice now. Two years ago, I did. Simple as that."

Nothing about him had ever been simple, she reflected. As for her feelings? Someday, someone might invent a word to describe them. Or him.

Long and lean, a little haunted, a lot more haunting, Aidan possessed a rather frightening ability to captivate. One look at his face and she'd tumbled—over the edge and straight down the slippery slope into love. Even after he'd "died," she hadn't climbed out.

Sighing, she tucked a leg underneath her on the bench. "Gaitor said you were the best he'd ever worked with."

"You haven't met his former partners."

She studied his unrevealing features before asking softly, "Why are you doing this? Trying so hard to downplay your abilities and disillusion me?"

"I'm not," he began, then raised his eyes as the lights winked off and on.

Unsure, Raven copied the move. "What? Electrical storms cause power flutters everywhere."

"Still a positive thinker, huh?"

Another double zap, and the crowd murmurs grew. Ignoring the shiver that chased itself over her skin, Raven glanced at the dusty bird next to her head. "They probably think Hezekiah's parasitic evil spirit is behind this."

Aidan smiled. "That's what they'd like to think, but Steven figures most of them are actually quite well educated."

"Mmm. Like people who hunt for vampires in grave-yards."

"You're never going to buy in, are you?"

"To the man-transforms-into-bird thing, not all the way in, no. To the suggestion that you're a coward, not at all."

"Raven, being stubborn about this won't change—"

A sizzling snap cut him off and sent a collective gasp through the suddenly pitch-black room.

"Hang on to your feathers," the owner called out. "We've got a generator…three, two, one, there she goes."

Less than a quarter of the lights sputtered back on. Grotesque shadows fell in all directions. Raven suspected it was a quiet order from the bartender that made the fiddle player pick up his bow and slide into a mournful East Coast lament.

"Old Joe knows how to create an atmosphere, I'll give him that." Twitching off a secondary shiver, Raven eased closer to Aidan. "Maybe we should leave."

A woman screamed. First one, then another, and another. Within seconds, a loud clatter of feet erupted, tables and chairs scraped across the floor, and people began to shout.

Raven's first instinct was to pinpoint the source of the commotion, but Aidan's hand on her neck prevented her from standing.

"I just want to see…" She swallowed the rest of that thought when two large, black shadows swooped down from the rafters.

The commotion swiftly bumped up to a full-scale panic.

"Under the table." Aidan took her there with him. "Do not leave this spot," he told her, and was gone before she could respond.

More fascinated than frightened, Raven watched several winged shadows move across the ceiling. "What is with the birds in this town?" she demanded of no one. "And that's not a raven, it's a crow."

A man running past tripped and sprawled on the bench she'd just vacated. A moment later, someone shoved a woman in leather sandals to the floor.

The fallen man scrambled to his feet and bolted. Raven crawled out from under the table to help the dazed woman. Blood oozed from a cut on her forehead, and she seemed disoriented.

Pressing a napkin to the wound, Raven asked, "How did this happen?"

In response, two pairs of stubby fingernails began to swipe the air between them. "He said they were possessed, and he was right."

"Who...? Ouch!" A heavy body slammed into Raven's shoulder. She heard flapping and saw a net fly into the air. There was a loud caw, and finally, the inevitable gunshot.

"We're damned." The woman, a shorn platinum-blonde, hiccuped. "Reverend Alley says we're going to burn in hell for our curiosity."

Of course there'd be a zealot in the mix. Keeping the woman low, Raven examined her forehead. "Cut's not deep." She caught the swiping hand before it scratched her face. "I promise, the birds won't hurt you if you stay right here."

"The evil needs a new host." Seriously drunk, the woman tipped sideways. "They never mentioned that in the brochure."

"Evil can be a bastard," Raven agreed. "Just stay here, okay, and that new host won't be you."

As another bullet discharged, she stood and attempted to locate Aidan and Rooney. A bullet could strike a human as easily as a bird. Aidan hadn't pulled the trigger, but he'd head straight for whoever had. And while Rooney wouldn't charge in, he'd be riveted enough by the spectacle not to leave.

Determined to get her great grandfather out, she started for the dartboard. And rammed straight into a man wearing a muscle shirt, biker gloves and a wicked leer.

"My, my, my," he drawled. "Ain't you just about the prettiest thing I've seen since that prison door swung open last month. What do you think, blondie? Is your friend here pretty enough to eat or what?"

The woman under the table launched into a sloppy hymn.

Firming his grip on Raven's wrists, the man let his leer widen. "I love these freako events. There's always some sugar begging to be sampled." He yanked her closer. "What say you and me step outside where we can be private with no birds to disturb us?"

His hold on her was painful and he smelled strongly of sweat and whiskey. At six-two, two hundred pounds, he wasn't as large as Fergus Smith, but right then, he seemed a great deal more menacing.

While she struggled, one of the ravens dived. The man ignored it and cinched her wrists tighter. Then he swore and swung her around beside him, into a one-armed throat lock that had her seeing spots.

"Take your holy book and beat it, preacher."

When her head cleared, Raven saw a second man standing placidly in front of them. A little bent and a lot scruffy, he sported a chest-length beard, thick glasses and a hat pulled low over his forehead.

"You leave her alone." The threat was clear even if his reedy voice barely carried over the confusion.

"Don't see a weapon anywhere." The arm around her

throat flexed, making it impossible for her to swallow. "You gonna hit me with your book if I don't obey?"

"It's an option," a smoother voice inserted from behind. "But I like my way better."

Aidan...

The man beside her made a sudden strangled sound. The bearded reverend melted quietly into the shadows.

"Let her go," Aidan advised her captor. "You've got two seconds before I drop you and let a bunch of panicking people use you as a floor mat."

"Bas—" The man choked, flexed his arm briefly, then released her with a shove.

Still behind him, Aidan tightened his sleeper hold on the biker. "You've got a lot of mean in you, pal." Dark eyes glinting, he snugged his forearm until the man's head lolled.

Raven massaged her abused windpipe. "Aidan."

"Bullies piss me off," he said, but shoved his prisoner into the wall and let go.

The man dropped to the floor.

"Are you hurt?" Aidan asked.

"No...bird," she cautioned, and dipped to avoid it.

Taking her hand, he drew her toward an as yet undiscovered side door. Raven grabbed the blonde under the table.

"It's a sign," the woman warbled. "The evil infected two people in the past, and it's ready to pestilitate...pestilent...Reverend Alley says it's gonna get someone again."

"Reverend Alley?" Aidan kept them moving.

"Fanatic," Raven told him. "Gotta be here for Ravenspell. He tried to help me."

"And there they are." Pausing, Aidan indicated three young men who were helping themselves to the money in the bar owner's cash drawer. "The instigators of tonight's bird drama."

Raven peered at the trio. "They look kind of...tough."

"They look it," he agreed. "Let's see if they act it."

"Interesting answer, Lieutenant."

Her speculative tone elicited a faint smile. "Three punks don't equal Johnny Demars." Aidan kicked the stuck exit door. "Get to the Jeep, and lock yourselves in. There's a robbery I need to screw up before we leave."

Raven tugged her hand free. "I'm not going anywhere without Rooney."

"Your hypothyroid server ushered him out first thing. Under protest, but he's long gone."

"Why do I feel like a less-than-great-granddaughter? Go," she told him, then pushed the blonde ahead of her. "I know where we parked."

"This way, ladies, if you please."

The bearded reverend startled her with his unexpected appearance. While Aidan went one-on-three with the thieves behind the bar, Raven found herself being propelled into a back lane where the shadows hung thick and unwelcoming.

Reverend Alley aimed a finger at Raven. "Take care, distant daughter of Hezekiah Blume. The evil that comes will surely seek you out. You and the man you love. You must be strong, have faith and, above all, be clever. Fail in any one of these areas, and you will die. Both of you will die. And mark me, this time the dying will be entirely real."

The woman sagged against Raven's arm as the reverend backed slowly away.

"Wait a minute," she said. Then lightning flashed and she caught a glimpse of his eyes.

His black, red-rimmed eyes.

NOT GOOD, RAVEN THOUGHT. Not necessarily real, but not something she'd needed to see after everything that had happened that night.

Red-rimmed eyes were her ancestor's affectation. Real or fake, they had no place in her life. On the other hand, this was Raven's Cove, where weird was more or less a synonym for normal.

After delivering the blonde to one of her camping companions, Raven went in search of her great-grandfather. Rooney was perched on the rear fender of the Jeep with a cane propped between his legs and several people milling around him.

"Doctor's here," he informed the gathering. He pointed from her to the people. "Patients are waiting."

"What? No, Grandpa, I can't..."

"Old Joe's bringing bandages and warm water. We already got your medical bag out of the backseat."

Raven noted an assortment of cuts and scrapes, saw more blood than she cared to and, relenting, knelt to check her equipment. "I don't suppose you found George in the backseat, as well."

Rooney made a rude sound. "Your so-called friend's gone. Took my Dodge pickup. Didn't ask, just took. But as long as he's hightailing it back where he belongs, I say good riddance and keep the truck. He's not your type, young Raven, not by a long shot."

"George isn't important, Grandpa. What matters is..."

"That our Aidan's alive?" The old man chortled. "Hell, I saw that with my own eyes inside."

She stared at him as Joe piled clean cloths and bandages in her arms. "You saw him, and it didn't strike you as odd?"

"Doesn't matter how it struck me, does it? What is, is. And right now, what is, is that these people need tending to. Nothing major, but if you want to set up shop in Raven's Cove, tonight's as good a time as any to dip your toe."

Absurd laughter tickled her throat. Could it get more unreal than this?

Aidan, a "dead" man, was inside a waterfront bar doing battle with a trio of thieves. A red-eyed reverend had just issued her a freakish warning. She had no idea where Steven or Fergus Smith had gone, although she imagined Steven might be watching the big man. George, whom she'd trusted for years, had stolen a truck and very likely chatted with the infamous Johnny Demars. And now here she stood, in a shadow-filled parking lot, with residual thunder still rumbling overhead, a strange kind of silvery fog rolling off the ocean, and a dozen wounded people in need of minor medical attention.

"Welcome to the Cove," she muttered, and finished rummaging through her bag.

She felt Aidan's presence behind her a second before he said, "Is this what you call locking yourself in the Jeep?"

Raven cast him a dry look. "Talk to Rooney." Then she looked again in disbelief.

His T-shirt was torn in three places. His hair had fallen over his forehead and into his eyes. He had a bruise on his cheekbone, a split lower lip, and the knuckles of his right hand were raw and bloody.

It amazed her that she could summon a casual "No cavalry, huh? Just you and the three toughies."

He shook out his sore fingers. "The police chief left office in July and hasn't been replaced yet. I'm told the deputy is indisposed and likely to remain so for several weeks."

She noticed that his eyes circled the parking lot before

returning to hers. Standing, she brushed the hair from his face. Couldn't help it. "You think Demars has someone here already, don't you?"

"I think he's probably close."

"And when he gets here, he'll do what Demars intended for him to do from the start."

Another visual circle. "We've had this conversation, Raven."

"No, we really haven't." Without looking back, she raised her voice to Rooney. "Tell everyone to line up, Grandpa. Most to least serious." The crowd sorted itself in some order. "We only had the conversation where Demars wanted you dead. But I don't think that's how it was." Although her stomach pitched, her voice remained dead calm. "Demars never planned to kill you, did he? He wanted you to live and suffer. It's like 'The Soldier's Tale,' Aidan. Not quite an eye for an eye, but close. You killed Demars's son. In return, Johnny Demars was going to kill me."

Chapter Six

"Demars's mother is Italian," Aidan revealed while she treated his scraped knuckles. "His gangland values— yeah, I know that's a contradiction in terms—come from the old school. No gratuitous killing. He targets specific victims for specific purposes. By eliminating the purpose, I eliminated his motive for targeting you."

Raven didn't know what to say to that, not then or fifteen minutes later when they arrived at the Ravenspell campsite.

An open fire burned high and wide beyond the rapidly expanding tent grounds as she struggled to absorb the truth behind Aidan's "death."

"You can yell at me if it makes you feel better, Raven." The object of her frustration draped an arm over her shoulders. "Or we could kickbox, and I'll give you first strike."

In spite of everything, his teasing tone brought a smile. "Such a tempting offer. When the Novocain impeding my brain function wears off, I might even take you up on it. In the meantime, and setting the big stuff aside, what are we doing here?"

"Hiding in a crowd for the moment."

"Hiding in, alone in—crowds appear to have multiple uses for you."

"I'm also hungry." He steered her toward a collection of lowered tailgates and the mouthwatering scents of grilled chicken, buttered corn and steamed clams. "If you spot Fergus Smith anywhere, give me a heads-up, because your cousin lost sight of him an hour ago."

"Steven's not a sleuth, and if you don't trust Fergus Smith, why not run an ID on him? My guess is you have open access Captain Beckett's computer."

"I had to earn some kind of income while I was here."

"And Steven facilitated that by—let me think—providing you with an internet connection at Blume House, maybe?"

"You have the mind of a first-class sleuth, angel. I've been investigating online scams and other fraud-related crimes."

"Not bad for a techno-spaz. Was that Captain Beckett's brainchild?"

Aidan chuckled. "His and mine. The man's not a monster, Raven. You let Gaitor poison your mind against him."

"In case you're not aware, Gaitor's been MIA since his retirement party, Aidan."

"Yeah, Beckett mentioned that."

"It's as if he dropped off the planet. Then again, you came back from the dead, so I'll hope for the best with Gaitor. Now, getting back to Fergus…"

"Fergus Smith from Bangor, Maine, or anywhere else for that matter, doesn't exist."

"There's a shock. Our Mr. Smith is a fraud. That would put him right up your alley—and let's not segue to a fanatical reverend of the same name. Any idea what Fergus's story might be?"

"No, but I'll figure it out eventually."

"Why doesn't that reassure me?"

"Because you're hungry, and lack of food makes you suspicious."

Raven settled for sending him a narrowed look.

It felt otherworldly, she realized as they walked, to be with Aidan like this, to have him touching her in such a familiar way, as if they'd never been apart.

She still loved him, desperately loved him. And wanted him. She should be tearing his clothes off and shoving him to the ground, or fantasizing about doing it. Instead, all she felt was numb. Is that what happened, she mused, when the human brain imploded?

At least her appetite was alive and well. And as Aidan had suggested, the mere prospect of food had improved her mood.

They blended in, loaded up two plates and ate on a fallen log, surrounded by tipsy legend hunters. Maybe it was a blessing, Raven thought, that they didn't see Fake Fergus, the blonde from the bar or the spooky Reverend Alley.

As the fire dimmed, a group of musicians began playing a Goth-folk musical mix on acoustic guitars. Mindless of the mosquitoes and the cooling night, a barefoot man with a long gray braid and beard produced a gallon jar filled with fruit and clear liquid, which he pushed into Raven's hands.

"Make you sleep like a baby," he promised. "Pass it on when you're done."

Aidan looked into the jar and grinned. "Make you see red-eyed ravens more like."

"Yes, about that." Raven sampled the home brew, felt the burn slide to her stomach and smiled. "Reverend Alley's eyes are red, or red-rimmed, anyway, like my ancestor's were after he transformed. Alley thinks that we—you and I—are going to die. He said so right before he went all raven eyed and poofed into the night."

"Sounds like a fun guy."

"He also knew my name, which would creep me out if my head wasn't processing so many other creepy thoughts." She popped a cube of overproof melon into her mouth. "Little things like Steven being disbarred and George selling you out." Pressing a slice of peach to his lips, she added a guileless "And of course there's the whole you sacrificing your life for me thing."

He swallowed the spiked fruit. "For us, Raven. There was no sacrifice involved as long as you were alive and safe."

She poured him a tall glass of the home brew. "I don't know how to respond to that, Aidan. Or to you. It's like I'm disconnected from my emotions right now. My feelings should be doing a happy dance, but instead, everything inside me's gone dark."

"And you think that makes you abnormal?"

"It makes me sad, which is ridiculous since you're sitting right here, and if a genie had popped out of a lamp to grant me a single wish, this—" she flicked a hand between them "—would be it."

"So substitute 'confused' for abnormal."

She drew random lines with her index finger. "My head's like a maze—no beginning, no end. Would you believe I wanted to open a medical clinic in Raven's Cove? I mean—that was the plan."

"It can still happen." With a vague smile hovering on his lips, he shot the contents of his glass. And hissed in reaction.

Humor sparked. "Rooney's tea packs a way bigger punch than this stuff. It's mother's milk, Aidan."

He frowned at the jar. "Probably just as well we never

had kids in that case. Then again, as I recall, you drank me under the table at our wedding reception."

"Must be in the genes. I'm pretty sure Rooney was weaned on malt whiskey." She passed the concoction to a couple sitting cross-legged on the grass in front of them. "Aidan, what will Demars do to George?"

"Depends how much he values a turncoat cop. Odds aren't in George's favor."

"Why did he turn you in?"

Aidan's lips took on an obscure curve. "I'll give you one guess. If it takes more than that, you're not the woman I married."

"A considerate man would let me live in denial." But she huffed out an impatient breath. "You think George is in love with me."

"I know he is. He was in love with you before I died. His coming to Raven's Cove tells me that situation hasn't changed."

"So he obviously saw you at Blume House this afternoon."

"I was on the staircase drooling while you were talking to Steven."

"After which, the three of us drove to Grandpa's cottage. George moved a few appliances, then contacted Demars. What he didn't count on was me going back to Blume House and finding you. Snap, there went his plan—if he actually had a plan." A familiar sensation swept over her from behind. "You know a break would be really nice, here. Do you feel something strange? Please say yes."

"Oh, yeah." Aidan kept his tone and movements easy as he swung a leg over to straddle the log. "I've been on it since we got here."

Fear and exasperation mixed. "You might have mentioned it before now."

"I could have been overreacting."

"Said Grandma to Red Riding Hood." She tapped a finger on his knee. "I hate to tell you your job, but shouldn't we be getting out of here?"

He took a long moment to scan the woods. "It's not one of Demars's men."

"And you know this because?"

The ghost of a smile appeared. "Sorry, gut instinct's the best answer I've got."

"If that's the same as cop instinct, I seem to recall the word *rusty* coming up earlier."

"Shakes your confidence a little, doesn't it?"

A movement in the mist caught her eye. "Someone's back there."

"Pretend he isn't."

When she opened her mouth, he wrapped his fingers around her nape and brought her forward for a kiss. Against her lips, he said, "You wouldn't see or feel him if it was Demars's man."

Raven promised herself to hold that thought, for as long as it took to absorb it. No one could smoke her mind with a kiss like Aidan.

"He's in the trees." Aidan drew back. "I'm going to give you a gun, and I need you to stay close behind me."

Although she disliked weapons, Raven took the compact Smith & Wesson he slipped into her hands. "I put seven stitches in a man tonight. Don't make me put a bullet in anyone."

"Do my best." He gave her a quick grin and an even quicker second kiss. "On three."

THE SINGING CAMPERS easily covered Aidan and Raven's departure from the site. Because Raven assumed they were taking a roundabout path to their destination, she kept quiet and kept up.

Although the forest floor was anything but level, it was also mossy enough that prayer and good balance kept her from falling on her face. Until they reached a patch of rocks, then her faith faltered.

"Stop. Down." Aidan tugged her into a crouch. "That huddled shadow's not part of any tree."

They'd come full circle to the campsite, Raven realized. Glittering firelight snuck through the greenery, but for the most part, the woods were a sea of mysterious shadows. She heard owls in the high branches, insects chirping, frogs croaking and God knows what else. If she spotted a wolf, big, bad or otherwise, she was out of here.

Aidan pointed. "Aim your gun at the base of the pine. If I yell at you to shoot, go for the stockier silhouette."

Really hating this, Raven thought, but she breathed out the worst of her nerves and set her wrists on a tree stump to steady them.

She didn't see Aidan leave, and she had no idea where he'd gone until the bloblike shadow near the pine tree vanished and the bone-on-bone punches that signaled a fight in progress began to underscore the night sounds.

Her heart hammered in her throat, and her fingers felt like blocks of ice. Finally, two distinct male shadows rose next to the pine. One of them howled and disappeared. The taller man went to his knee.

"It's okay, Raven. I've got him."

She forced her screaming muscles to relax, stood and made her way to Aidan's side.

The fallen figure took on a recognizable form. "George." Disappointment flooded out. "I'd hoped we were wrong. Stupid, but I hoped."

The distant campfire allowed her to see the tears that shone on his cheeks when he looked at her.

"I didn't mean for this to happen, Raven. I called Demars before I realized what he might do to you."

Aidan hauled him upright. Defeated, George wiped at the dirt that streaked his face. "I'm sorry, Aidan." His mouth and eyes crumpled. "I really am so sorry. I saw you come out of the bar so I followed you up here. I wanted to tell you, to warn you."

"Who did he send?" Aidan asked.

"I don't know the guy's real name. He's called Weasel. His blood's ice water. He carries a knife, but he's a marksman."

"You seem to know Demars's shooters very well," Raven noted. "How long have you worked for him?"

George flinched. "I don't work for him, not really. I pass along the odd bit of information. Very odd and very much in bits." He appealed to Aidan. "I thought he'd killed you. I thought he might decide to kill me, for being with you the night his son died. I wanted— I was trying to protect myself."

"Right. Let us know how that goes."

"Can I... Are you going to let me leave?"

For an answer, Aidan held up both hands and stepped away.

"The guy looks like what he's called." George edged backward. "You won't mistake him. And watch for the big guy, too. I haven't actually met him, but you hear things. I know Demars wants you dead very, very badly."

It surprised Raven that she heard the tiny *thwack,* but she did. Heard it and saw the expression of shock that froze George's features. With a dark stain blooming across his T-shirt, he pitched forward to land facedown on the moss.

Raven and Aidan hit the ground at the same instant.

A second later, Aidan pulled her partway up. "Keep low and keep moving, okay?"

She nodded, or thought she did.

He shielded her from behind and stayed there until they reached the campfire where thirty or more people continued to debate the ancient tale.

"He's dead." Raven fisted Aidan's shirt, holding on even when he pulled her into his arms. "George is dead."

"Yeah, he's dead." Pressing his cheek to the side of her head, he held her tight. "What I don't get is why we're not."

THE QUESTION HAUNTED him through the remainder of a sleepless night.

They returned to Blume House, to the attic rooms that had been his sanctuary since the explosion. He knew all the ways in, and he'd added an extra way out.

Raven would be safe here for now, and he'd have time to think—about her was a given, since she was currently sleeping in his bed. After two years with nothing for company except memories of the nights they'd spent together, and the spectacular sex they'd shared, he'd worry a whole lot more if he wasn't ready to crawl and beg.

However, focus was key at this point. Lose it, and he risked losing Raven forever.

Leaving the trapdoor open, Aidan hauled himself into the cupola and surveyed the darkened ridge. When his cell phone vibrated, he barely glanced at the screen. "Where are you?"

Steven's cranky voice replied, "Two flights down and climbing. I figured I'd give you a heads-up in case you decided to blow mine off before doing a visitor ID."

"Don't wake Raven."

"Aidan, dynamite won't wake Raven if she's asleep."

"Yeah." The memory brought a smile. "Only two cups of strong coffee can do that."

Sixty seconds later, Steven flung himself into a bean-bag chair.

"I can hear your teeth grinding from here." Aidan didn't have to see the other man's expression to know what had happened. "How much did you lose?"

"Five K."

"Gotta be a record, even for you."

"You'd think so, wouldn't you? Don't tell Rooney."

"That shouldn't be a hard promise to keep."

"Or Raven."

"Uh-huh. Like she won't figure it out. Lucky for you, you're too low on her life-and-death priority list to get the verbal crap kicked out of you. You were supposed to be watching Fergus Smith, Steven, not losing what's left of your personal assets in an online poker match."

"Yeah, about that. Mr. Not-His-Real-Name Smith might be the size of a humpback whale, but he moves like an eel. He ditched me in the vicinity of Two Toes Joe's bar. I figured if he went inside, you'd see him, and if he didn't, we'd have a better chance of finding him when the fog that was rolling in rolled out and the sun— assuming we live long enough to see it again—came up. Because my guess is that Johnny Demars must be working a gargantuan chip at this juncture, and he might not settle for offing you and Raven. He might want anyone and everyone remotely connected to you and her gone. Is that just barely possible?"

"Barely," Aidan agreed.

"Ambiguity is not an answer." Steven raked the fingers of both hands through his hair. "Give me something solid, will you? What are we looking at here?"

Aidan weighed choice against risk before deciding. "I need to see the body."

"Body?" Only Steven's eyes came up. "As in dead body?"

"Very dead. One of Demars's sharpshooters took George out of the picture in the woods near the Ravenspell campsite."

"He took… Does that even make sense?"

"It does to whoever squeezed the trigger."

"Man, I need a beer. Where were you and Raven when this taking out occurred?"

"Sandwiching George."

"So the double dealer died, and you and Raven walked. Call me dense, but I'd say whoever did your former police bud is definitely not working for Johnny Demars…. Wait a minute. What are you doing?"

After checking his gun, Aidan stuffed an extra ammo clip in his pocket and tossed his backup to Steven. "I can't leave a corpse in the woods. One of the campers might take an early-morning stroll." He tugged on a black jacket. "Watch Raven. I'll be back in an hour."

Steven was up like a shot. "Are you insane? How do you know you're not walking into a trap?"

"If George's killer wanted me dead, I'd be dead. So would Raven. We got lucky tonight, and I'm damned if I know why. Yet."

"Trap," Steven called out as he left the cupola.

The prospect hung with him during his jog through the woods to the spot where George had landed.

Except that George was no longer in the spot where he'd landed. Close, but not in quite the same place. Or the same position.

Running his penlight over the corpse, Aidan replayed the scene.

George had fallen on his stomach. Now he was lying on his side. He'd been dead when he'd hit the ground. His facial expression hadn't altered, and the blood flow indicated a major arterial strike. Obvious answer? Someone had moved him.

Aidan regarded the now-quiet clearing. If a camper had discovered the body, Rooney would have heard the furor three miles away in his seaside cottage. This movement was the killer's doing.

He located George's wallet. There was one debit and two credit cards inside. He had a Milky Way zipped into his jacket pocket, along with a factory-sealed pack of condoms. He also had the photo of Raven that Aidan had kept front and center on his work desk.

Okay, well it wasn't like he hadn't known. Didn't have to like it, but he'd known.

He turned the body back to its original position and only spotted the small tear in the fabric because the collar of George's jacket was turned up.

The sight of it brought to mind another time and place—and another torn collar.

Four summers ago, he and Gaitor had discovered a man buried in a Milwaukee Dumpster. The man, a police informant, had worked for Johnny Demars. A fresh round of information concerning one of Demars's hit men had been passed to Gaitor earlier that night.

Further investigation had turned up a listening device. According to forensics, the clip that had attached the device to the dead man's collar had caused the tear.

All of which added up to a probable second listening device, likely planted on an unsuspecting George by Demars's sharpshooter, and removed in a rush later.

George had called the guy Weasel. George had also

done an about-face and come to warn them, or at least warn Raven, about what he'd done.

Demars didn't trust anyone, and he didn't give second chances. George had been toast the minute he'd opened his mouth to them in the woods.

Exhaling slowly, Aidan stood. He'd wanted to know why only one person had died tonight, and now he did.

He just wished it hadn't been the worst possible answer.

Chapter Seven

The dream slid through Raven's sleeping mind in much the same way as the night fog moved through the Cove—with insidious purpose and a serpentine quality that chilled her blood.

Red-rimmed eyes watched her; she felt them on her skin like points of ice. Looking up, she spied Hezekiah in bird form. He was perched in a tall tree, waiting, she supposed, for another death. Reverend Alley also watched her, but he was farther away, standing alone among the high ridge rocks, and not an active threat at the moment.

Danger resided ahead of her, in the form of two male silhouettes. One wore a black executioner's hood, the other wore black everything.

She recognized Aidan instantly and tried to call his name. But no sound emerged from her throat, and her feet had taken root on the stony ground.

"An eye for an eye." The hooded man's whisper was as clear as if he'd spoken the words directly into her ear. She saw his mad smile through the hood even as something long and sinuous began to twine around her frozen limbs.

"How selfless of you, Raven, to want to save your husband as he attempted to save you. Do you recall your great-grandfather's telling of 'The Soldier's Tale'?"

Only her throat muscles loosened. "A convalescing

World War I veteran killed the man he believed to be responsible for the death of his brother."

"It should have been a brother for a brother dead. Unfortunately, it didn't work out that way." The smile became a hideous parody. "In our time, however, that minor problem can be set right. My son is dead, and I mourn the loss. Your husband tried and failed to protect you. Now you've come to save him. An intriguing trade-off, and one you'll ultimately win. I stand by my plan. Aidan mourns the loss. An eye for an eye."

As if levitated by a magician's hand, Raven began to float toward the edge of the cliff.

She struggled but couldn't break her invisible bonds. She'd almost reached the rim when someone knocked her from the air. She landed on a body and was quickly rolled onto her back.

Aidan, looking dark and dangerous, stared down at her. "Whatever this part of the legend was supposed to be, Raven, I won't let you die. If we have to play it out, we'll play it like 'The Soldier's Tale.' Not a true eye for an eye."

She fisted the front of his shirt. "I don't want to lose you again, Aidan. Don't make…"

Like a light snapping off, the ridge went dark. Everyone and everything winked out. Every sound disappeared. Until all that remained was the frantic pulsing of her heart and a wispy voice that echoed in her head.

"Death is not the end of this evil journey, Raven Blume. In this place, death is the beginning.…"

THE FOG BURNED OFF by midmorning. Which was about how long it took Raven to relegate the lingering effects of her dream to the realm of fantasy where they belonged.

Because he knew and understood her, Aidan made coffee, then waited across the room while she drank it.

"I can't hide in an attic and play solitaire until this nightmare is resolved." Unsure why her frustration was building instead of diminishing, she frowned out the dormer window. "How can a sunny day give such a strong impression of dark?"

"There's another cloud mass moving in." Aidan's lips twitched as she rooted through her suitcase. "Until it arrives, I'd go with short shorts and a really skimpy top."

To her surprise, and minor relief, Raven's insides trembled. Apparently she wasn't as disconnected from her emotions today as she had been last night. Now if the danger would only blow away or at least drop to an acceptable level, she might be able to encourage her feelings instead of pushing them back.

The temperature had fallen substantially overnight. In response, Raven drew out a pair of skinny jeans, slouchy boots and a snug-fitting white cotton tee. It wasn't until she was safely behind the bathroom door that she released a breath and looked in the mirror.

Pale, hazy features stared back at her. She hadn't seen this version of herself since Aidan's funeral. Going with that, she let her mind drift past his "death," to a less turbulent time in her life.

They'd lived in a downtown Milwaukee apartment after their wedding. Just the two of them and Dublin, a black cat Aidan had found at the end of a long shift.

Those had been happy times, for all of them.

Aidan had touched her in a way no other man ever had or could. He'd stared at her with his hypnotic eyes and kissed her with his amazing, inventive mouth. He'd run his hands over her body and electrified her skin. He'd made her fall so deeply in love with him there'd been no way out. Then he'd gone to a ball game with friends, stopped at a convenience store—and been forced to die.

The color of her world had altered the moment Aidan's partner had arrived on her doorstep. She remembered how he'd stood there, a gray, brittle man, so much older than he'd been the day before.

"They didn't tell you, either, did they, Gaitor?" she murmured. "And now you're somewhere—I hope you're somewhere—probably still blaming yourself for an explosion that never happened."

An explosion that never happened, her brain echoed….

Aidan wasn't dead. She'd been granted a miracle. So why did the lie behind it hurt so much?

Because no matter how miraculous the discovery, Raven knew that if she hadn't come to Maine, she might never have learned he was alive. She would have lived her life in various stages of mourning. Moved on eventually, but that huge, hollowed-out part of her would have remained empty forever.

Knowing Aidan would knock soon and check on her, she turned on the shower in the tiny stall. Rolling the tension from her neck, she waited for hot water, then hung her robe and stepped under the spray.

They'd had sex in stalls much smaller than this. Truly great sex that made her knees turn to rubber and her nipples go hard.

Not helpful, Raven, she thought. No matter how tempting, she couldn't allow the prospect of phenomenal shower sex to top her priority list. Even the recollection of it had no business being there.

A hired killer was the priority here. And a dead friend—or, well, not really friend, but still—dead.

Out of the shower and dry, she slathered on a layer of body cream, left her long hair damp and seriously hoped a second cup of coffee would make things clearer to her.

"You look like a woman who wants to bite someone's

head off. I'm guessing mine, since we're alone." Aidan masked the grin, but not quite the humor in this tone. "Tells me you've been thinking too much."

Raven controlled an urge to snarl and refilled her mug. "Did you know that neither of Gaitor's ex-wives has any idea where he is?"

Before he could respond, she gave a false smile and said at the same time as him, "Yeah, I heard about that."

He cocked his head. "You have a very spooky talent there, angel. Not only do you nail the words, but you also hit the timing dead on."

She drank and felt marginally more cheerful. "Rooney says it's a quirk that goes hand in hand with my ability to diagnose unusual medical conditions. He thinks I pick up on seemingly insignificant physical signals. In this case, the barely perceptible change in your expression as I finished making the statement."

He stared. "Jesus, Raven. That theory's as spooky as the quality." He nodded at her purse. "I used your iPhone to check something out. Hope you don't mind."

"Why would I mind?"

"Because part of you is still pissed at me, and Dublin's claws have nothing on yours when they're out."

She sent him an artless smile. "Dublin's good, if that was your way of asking. He's visiting my mother, who swears he's the reincarnation of one of our less infamous Blume ancestors." Another sip did the trick. "Who did you call, and why not use your own phone? Never mind. Leopard, spots. You forgot to charge it. But I'm still curious about the who part."

"You could say I was playing a hunch with reference to an old friend."

"Meaning Gaitor or Captain Beckett… Oh, God. You called George's number, didn't you?"

"His cell phone was missing when I went back last night."

"Okay." She considered that. "Any luck?"

"It was a shot in the dark. Unfortunately, I wasted a bullet."

"A no would have done there, but speaking of shots and darkness, is it possible that Weasel got hold of the bearded hippie guy's Mason jar before he pulled the trigger, and that's why George is gone and we're not?"

"More likely, George was simply a lackey who'd served his purpose."

"Terrific. So when's it our turn?"

Pushing off from the half-shuttered window, Aidan walked slowly toward her. His dark eyes were steady, his movements smooth, the hair that framed his gorgeous features much longer than it had been two years ago.

"I figure soon. Demars will want to finish this in Raven's Cove."

Raven held her ground, but tipped her head back when he stopped in front of her. "Seeing as that's what you want, too, wish granted, it appears. On both sides."

He slid his thumb over her chin. "Except both sides can't win, and we've already forfeited more than our fair share."

She wasn't breathing properly, Raven realized, wasn't thinking at all. The look in his eyes said he wanted her. But even something as simple as a kiss would lead straight to the bed she'd slept in last night. And she wasn't there yet, in her head. Almost, but not all the way. "Aidan, I need…"

"I know." He lowered his mouth to hers. Didn't touch, but she felt the warmth of his breath and, under her hand, the uneven beat of his heart. "If you could forget a two-year nightmare in less than a day, you wouldn't be the woman I fell in love with in a grungy city alley over a bunch of dented trash cans."

Because it was the last thing she'd expected him to say, she laughed and gave him a light push. "We did not fall in love over trash cans."

"Maybe you didn't, but that's when I took the plunge."

"Love was the last thing on my mind that night. I'd just lost my purse and laptop to a junked-up little creep."

"You might have lost a whole lot more if Gaitor and I hadn't witnessed the robbery."

"The creep mugged me and took off. There was no suggestion of rape."

"I think you whacking him with a metal trash can lid might have factored into that."

She widened expressive eyes. "It was a brand-new laptop. Plus, I'd already seen you and Gaitor at the back door of the bar. When my friend screamed, Gaitor waved his badge and shouted that you were cops. Of course I was going to try and bash the guy. Okay, credit where it's due, two minutes later, you had the mugger pinned to the ground, and I had my purse and laptop back. I was grateful, yes, but not in love."

Grinning, he let her nudge him back another step. "I heard you, Raven. You told your friend you wished it was you on the ground instead of the junkie who'd robbed you."

"Your ego needs a hearing aid, pal. My classmate said that, not me."

"Like hell."

She wouldn't laugh, she promised herself, but she had to swallow to keep it from slipping out. "She said it, Aidan. I only thought it. Once. Briefly." She gave in to a smile. "All right, fine, maybe I was a little smitten, but, come on, seriously, do the math. Gorgeous cop, major rescue, impressionable med student…"

"Beautiful med student."

"Uh-huh." Still smiling, she crammed her iPhone into the pocket of his jeans. "I heard you and Gaitor talking afterward. That takedown was pure cop reflex. You saw me and everyone else through a fog that night."

With amusement still hovering, he returned to the window and glanced at the courtyard. "You have a mean memory, sweetheart."

"I do, and the scary thing is, it's nothing compared to Steven's." The humor faded. "Or Johnny Demars's, apparently. Aidan, tell me the truth, why didn't we die with George?"

"I'd say either Weasel's a crappy shot or he has a different agenda than the one we anticipated."

"That's only half an answer."

"If you're smart, you'll take it and be satisfied."

"If I was smart, I'd have listened to Steven and become a cosmetic surgeon. Look, I get that Weasel shot George and let us go because those were his orders, I just don't understand why…"

It slammed into her, like one of the previous night's lightning bolts, hard, fast and with a jolt that raced from her brain straight to her nerve ends.

"Those were his orders," she repeated. "To get rid of George and leave us alone. My God, it really is a spin on the eye for an eye adage. You pulled the trigger that killed Johnny Demars's son." Her head came up. "In return, Johnny Demars is going to pull the trigger that kills me."

AIDAN UNDERSTOOD RAVEN'S need to move. He also knew she was going to fire a stream of questions at him while they did.

The first came when they reached the third floor hallway. "Does Beckett know where Demars is?"

"Someone suggested Bangkok."

"Better than Bangor, I suppose. Do you have even a vague description of the man?"

"Gort," he replied. "Cold, faceless, powerful—it's all we know."

"Age?"

"Somewhere between forty and sixty is the going guess."

"Is Demars his real name?"

"No."

"I'm sensing a dead end here. New direction. Why was his kid such a screwup?"

"Why did the chicken cross the road?" Her hiss had him setting his hands on her shoulders and directing her toward the staircase ahead. "Jason's bad wasn't the same as Johnny's. He came out of a black hole twelve years ago. We'd hoped to use him to locate his father, but no luck there. Jason stayed out of the hole and caused trouble. Johnny stayed in it, and did what he could to keep his kid from doing any hard time."

Raising her hands, Raven started down the stairs. "I give up. Faceless, ageless, possibly in Bangkok, had a screwed-up kid he couldn't control. Do you want to hear something totally crazy?"

"You're going to give up medicine and cast runes like your mother?"

He saw her smug amusement. "My mother makes good money playing to her strength. And if you say her strength is being spacey, I promise you, when this nightmare's done, I'll get her to show you one of her less male-friendly talents."

"Not a promising prospect, I'll admit, but I'm glad

you think we'll live long enough for a threat like that to be carried out."

"Call it my faith in your strength. As for the crazy something I mentioned…"

"You want to have sex in a shadowy stairwell?"

Her smile sent a surge of blood straight to his groin. "Well, duh, Aidan, that's not crazy, it's just us recreating a scene from our first vacation together in Istanbul."

"It was an elevator in Istanbul."

"It went up and down like a stairwell."

"It was a hundred years old. It got stuck more often than it ran."

"Making it the perfect setting for a sex-hungry couple to use as a launching pad for the wild ride that their lives ultimately became. Can we go back to crazy?"

"If the sex thing's a bust, yeah."

They emerged into a first-floor utility room that smelled like old roses. Long, narrow shadows became wide, angular ones. Raven continued to lead, which suited Aidan fine since walking behind her gave him an excellent view of her truly superior ass.

"I've been weighing it out," she said over her shoulder. "And I've come to the conclusion that I'm as curious as I am terrified to see Johnny Demars's face. Because, really, how many people who are alive can claim to have done that? I know many have, but how many of those many can say they knew who it was they were seeing?"

Aidan rested his shoulder on a wall while she jiggled an ancient key in an even more ancient lock. "Wading through all of that, I'd speculate not many. Rumor has it Demars's wife disappeared a dozen or so years ago, and he only had the one kid."

"Maybe his mother's vanishing act triggered Jason's rebellious behavior. Did anyone ever meet her?"

"We had an informant once who did."

"And you didn't get this informant to give you a description of Johnny Demars because…?"

"He refused to do it. Out of fear, I imagine. Justified as it turns out. Gaitor and I found his body in a Dumpster. Like George, one bullet did the job. In the informant's case, that bullet entered the body through his mouth."

"Point made, but—well, ew."

"Dead's dead, Raven. His death was just messier than some."

Reaching down, he punched the obstinate lock. When the door opened, she smiled and dropped the key in his hand. "It's entirely possible you chose the wrong line of work, Lieutenant."

"Thought's crossed my mind."

The air felt dank and heavy in what Raven instantly identified as a medical amphitheater. Four rows of wooden desks stepped upward from a large oval pit. Overhead, two of ten lights flickered precariously.

"Not sure I'd have felt inspired to learn in a place like this." She turned a stationary circle. "Still—different time. I can't see setting up a clinic here."

Two insignificant chambers later, they entered a large library. Filthy books crammed three walls of shelves. Cobwebbed plates and teacups sat on dusty tables. There was a pipe propped up next to an ashtray and a magazine lying open on the window seat.

"It's like the *Mary Celeste*." Raven stepped over a pair of men's slippers. "Do you have any idea which wing we're in?" Her head came up. "Did you hear something?"

A cautious creak reached them. Aidan listened to the extended tread and felt anticipation rise.

Raven's eyes slitted. "Why do you look more stoked than worried?"

"One guess. But in case I'm wrong." He handed her his second gun.

The usual precautions applied. However, when he booted the door open and hit the light switch, he saw what he'd expected.

Massive sneakers in hand, a tiptoeing Fergus Smith blinked once, then stared like an animal caught in headlights.

Aidan ran his gaze around a mostly empty parlor. "Bathroom outside didn't work for you, huh?"

"Actually…"

"How's your mother doing?"

"She's not…she's…aw, hell." Shoulders slumping, the big man deflated. "There's no one here but me. Oh, hello." He peered past Aidan to smile warily at Raven. "My name's not Smith, it's Fanning. Fergus Fanning."

The name rang a distant bell in Aidan's head. "Why are you in Raven's Cove?"

Sock footed, Fergus toed the floor dust. "Someone I know needed a favor. I needed some cash."

"Give me a name."

"Er, all I can tell you is he'd have come himself if he could've."

"He?"

"My uncle."

The bell clanged, finally. Fanning. Christ. Of course. "You're Gaitor's nephew."

Beside him, Raven's expression went from puzzled to surprised to delighted. "Gaitor's alive?" Every part of her lit up. "Where is he, Fergus, do you know?"

"Not exactly. Last we talked, he was following a lead. He said Demars might live in Wisconsin, but there's no way he confines all his dirty work to that state." Relieved, he glanced at the pocket of Aidan's jeans. "I think that's you ringing."

Raven smiled. "My phone, my call."

She dug it out—something Aidan didn't mind at all—and regarded the screen.

"It's Rooney." Pressing Talk, she turned away. "Hi, Grandpa."

"I didn't mean any harm," Fergus insisted. "Truth is, that's what I was supposed to prevent. My uncle's been worried sick about Raven since you died—which he really thought you'd done. He figured Demars might be keeping an eye on her, so he—my uncle's—been doing the same."

Before Aidan could respond, Raven spun back. "No, stay right there…we're on our way. We have to go," she told him. "Someone broke into Rooney's cottage and locked him in the bathroom."

"Is he hurt?"

"He says no, but he also says whoever did it took his wallet, his gold pocket watch…" Fearful eyes locked on his. "And Steven."

Chapter Eight

"He stuck a gun to my head and told me I could either walk into the bathroom under my own steam, or he'd throw me in with a bullet in my brain."

Raven had to duck or be hit with the baleful hand Rooney flung.

"I told him right back he wouldn't be so cocky if he'd made that threat forty years ago. Told him I boxed right up to my sixtieth birthday, and by God, I was good at it. Got advice more than once from old Rocky himself."

Aidan, who'd been examining the lock on the cottage door, glanced up. "You knew Rocky Marciano?"

"You bet I did. I was at the Boston Garden the night he…"

"Knocked out George McInnis. Save that one, Grandpa, for the party we'll throw when we get Steven back." Raven pulled the stethoscope from her medical bag. "Tell us what happened here this morning. Did you see the man who threatened you?"

"'Course I did. I'm not blind, you know."

"Stop pushing at my hand. I need to check your heart."

"Sound as a dollar," he muttered, but let her listen.

A smile touched her lips at the steady beat. "I guess thieves and kidnappers don't scare you much, huh?"

"Not a whole lot scares me at my age." Giving a feeble

cough, Rooney used his eyes to motion Aidan toward the counter and his collection of mugs.

Raven waved the blood pressure cuff in his face. "Uh, Grandpa, I'm right here. At least wait until I'm preoccupied before you encourage Aidan to facilitate your bad habit. And yes, I know how old you'll be next month. We should all live so long, including my pain-in-the-butt cousin who better not be hurt."

"He's not. The little turd shoved him down and pointed his gun, but I heard two sets of boots walking out the door."

"Did he say anything?" Aidan picked up the pot of tea Rooney had brewed before they'd arrived.

"Said he liked my watch, and he wasn't about to say no to free money. Looked like a ferret," the old man spit. "Smelled like a skunk."

While her great-grandfather supplied the details of Weasel's appearance, Raven took his pulse. Seventy-six and regular. Looking from Aidan to the teapot, she made a go-ahead gesture. "Why would Weasel take Steven?" she wondered aloud. "I'm pretty sure money isn't spilling from my cousin's pockets these days."

"Think Johnny Demars and intent," Aidan suggested.

It only took her a second to put the two things together. "Well, that's just low." Intercepting the mug, she took an irritated sip and was amazed her throat didn't burst into flames.

"It's my never-fail tonic," Rooney defended. He swallowed a larger mouthful without flinching. "Now explain what you just said."

Aidan grinned. "Your great-grandfather, Raven, your explanation."

She breathed out the residual heat. "Demars wants to make sure Aidan and I stay in the Cove. Steven's family…he's been kidnapped…ergo, we won't leave until he's home and safe." She raised her voice to Demars's invisible hit man. "Not that we'd have left town anyway, seeing as I'm distantly related to three-quarters of the people in it."

Aidan's grin widened. "Two Toes Joe?"

"Second cousin, once removed."

"Hezekiah's her eight times great-grandfather," Rooney stated with pride. "Raven and Lacey and me are his most direct kin."

Raven shone a penlight into his eyes. "You might not want to mention that connection to Reverend Alley, Grandpa."

Rooney snorted. "Heard about that old spook. I figure on meeting him before Ravenspell ends."

Aidan ran his gaze around the room. "Makes two of us."

"I'm glad you're both feeling so sociable." Raven re-packed her bag. "Can we get back to Steven now?"

If Aidan had a plan—doubtful in her opinion—he had no chance to explain it. Two trucks squealed to a halt outside, followed by a van and three cars. People Raven had never met poured into the kitchen. They carried pitchers, casserole dishes and platters heaped with sandwiches they would cheerfully have exchanged for Weasel's head.

Aidan vanished with the first wave, no surprise there, leaving Raven to deal with a cottage full of outrage and local gossip.

When she inquired about the police force, a woman in cat's-eye glasses pulled her aside. "You know the Cove's a series of terraces, right? Buildings cling to the cliff and literally step down to the water. Well, Caleb Weaver—he's the deputy—went to break up a dogfight a couple nights back. When the barking was done, old

Caleb wound up taking the fast way from the post office down to cousin Rhonda's bakeshop. You'd think the stupid fool would know better. Put a foot wrong on those stone stairs, and you'll be rolling all the way to the harbor. Bottom line? Our deputy's out of commission for the next six to eight weeks with a broken leg."

"Where is he now?" Raven asked above the growing noise.

The woman, apparently her fourth cousin, pushed a lemon square into her hands. "My husband took him to the hospital in Bangor. He'll hole up there long as he can, eat as much of their food as he can and when the doctors and nurses get sick of him, which won't be long, he'll come back and make us feed him until Christmas. That—" she tapped Raven's arm for emphasis "—is why we need a clinic here in the Cove."

"So, I'll be responsible for feeding him from now until Christmas." Something hard jabbed Raven's hip from behind. Looking down, Raven followed the line of her great-grandfather's cane to his favorite kitchen chair.

She made her way over, cursing Aidan all the way. If he loved her, he'd have taken her with him when he escaped. She sighed and crouched. "What is it, Grandpa?"

The old man tapped his nose. "Remember I said the thief smelled like a skunk? Well, I just got wind of your cousin Emma who makes candles and such for her shop on the steps. She does those little cone things now as well. The ones you burn."

"Incense?"

"That's it, that's how the scumbag smelled."

"Like incense."

"Just like it. And here's the kicker. Emma rents out the apartment over her shop. Been vacant for a year." A wily smile crept over Rooney's face. "Until last night."

RAVEN'S COUSIN DROVE ahead of them along a series of winding outer roads to her quaint step-side shop. A seventysomething hippie, she had a waiflike body and the face of an aging angel. The minute Aidan climbed out of the Jeep, she marched over to inform him that if she found Weasel first, she'd roast his balls on a spit for hurting Rooney. Then she smiled, took them inside and pointed at the apartment door.

"I smelled something coming down the stairs when I opened the shop this morning. Go on in, and see what I found."

A collection of twenty-plus take-out containers littered the wood floor. Raven counted three cola and six beer bottles, a dozen candy bar wrappers and a mostly eaten round of Limburger cheese.

Aidan sniffed one of the boxes. "Onion rings."

"And chow mein, and fried rice, and pot stickers and some kind of gooey stuff with orange sauce on it." As she sifted through the mess, Raven spied something small and white on a piece of foil. "Aw, look. Goldilocks left us a gift."

Aidan checked out the view from the window. "Explains the munchies, anyway." He walked over to crouch beside her. "Food'll be local. We can ask around, see what we come up with."

Emma's eyes brightened. "Or you could set a trap. Rusty leghold would be my choice."

Standing, Raven dusted off. "As you see, mean runs a true and steady course through most of the family. I'm afraid that after manhandling Rooney, mercy isn't a thing Weasel's likely to get."

"I'll take that as a warning to stay on the good side of your family. Has this sort of thing happened before?" Aidan asked Emma.

"Twice this past year. Never with so much food, though. And talk about nerve. Last night's intruder took a shower before he left. That's just plain crazy, you ask me."

"It's something," Aidan agreed.

When he walked away, Emma elbowed Raven's side. "So is this your man, or just a cop in town for Ravenspell?"

"He's…"

"Hell of a looker why ever he's here. Has a real Hezekiah aura about him. Leaning toward bad, but not so far he couldn't be pulled back."

"He has his moments of bad." Raven rubbed her bruised ribs. "But the cop side usually wins out."

"I think we're done here." Returning, Aidan treated Emma to a smile that earned Raven another hard elbow. "Lock the place through Ravenspell, and you should be fine."

"Bring me the slimeball who knocked Rooney around, and I'll be better. I still know where I hid my daddy's old bear traps. They should be plenty horrible by now. Skewered slimeballs," she added, spacing the words for effect.

"Paints a picture, doesn't it?" Raven remarked when they were back outside.

"Yeah, and being a guy, it's not one I care to contemplate." Aidan took her hand on the crooked stone stairway that bisected the town. "It wasn't Weasel who broke in."

"I knew you were going to say that. Why?"

"Did you smell any incense up there?"

"Not a bit."

"And yet Emma could smell the leftover food in her shop. Air flows down in that building. Makes the apartment livable no matter what business is in residence below. If Weasel smelled of incense as Rooney claims, it didn't come from here."

"There was a lot of food up there, too. No one person could eat that much."

"No Weasel-size person."

"Then who…?" Raven's foot slipped, and took the question with it. Only Aidan's arm circling her waist prevented a reenactment of the deputy's late-night roll down the stairs.

The contact didn't startle so much as remind Raven of what she'd been missing for the past two years. Lean by nature, Aidan was all sinew and sleek muscle under his clothes, all heat and energy under his skin. If it had been about lust and nothing else, she would have jumped him in a heartbeat.

So why not do it? she reflected. Why not let her hormones take over, go back to Blume House and have sex until one or both of them were too exhausted to continue?

True, her head was still a quagmire, but in the grand scheme, they were married, and, face it, she wanted him—almost enough to take him right here.

A sigh slipped out. Too bad about the "almost."

"We could ask Emma to let us borrow the upstairs apartment," Aidan suggested.

"What?" Tuning back in, Raven realized that his mouth was a tantalizing inch away from hers. And her hand, God, it was sliding over the front of his jeans. On the stone stairs. In full view of every tippy little shop that lined them.

Wincing slightly, she eased her fingers away. But when she tried to sidestep, Aidan merely tightened his grip and smiled.

"Need a moment here, sweetheart, to wind down from what neither of us probably meant to start. It doesn't take much to make me react to you right now."

Although it was both dangerous and stupid, Raven

shimmied her hips against him, then laughed at the gleam that sprang into his eyes. "Looks like your famous cop control needs work, McInnis. And you know me, always happy to oblige a person in need."

"Practice makes perfect?"

"If that works for you."

"You know, it really doesn't. But I'll show you what does." He took her mouth before she could respond.

As instantly aroused as she was staggered by his action, Raven absorbed the sensations that raced through her bloodstream.

Now this was some kind of kick-ass kiss. Need punched through logic and slammed into desire. Something stronger than hunger clawed in her belly.

She felt every part of him digging into her, burning her skin and driving her up. This was no taste of what had been, it was an out-and-out assault on her system. It was astonishing. It was incredible.

It was insanity!

She managed—no idea how since most of her brain cells had been stunned into a coma—to drag her mouth free. "Aidan, we're on full voyeuristic display here."

"You think?"

No, not at all. She understood that much. Thinking was precisely what she hadn't done before starting this.

When his lips covered hers again, she knew she should twist her head away and make him stop. But it felt so amazing to be with him again, to rediscover everything she thought she'd lost.

He smelled like the rain and fog at night. He tasted like coffee and sex. If her back hadn't come up against a wall, she thought she might never have surfaced.

Fortunately, the impact jarred her enough that her

brain kick-started itself. "Aidan..." she began again, then paused and raised her eyes. "Why is it so dark?"

He kept his own eyes on her mouth. "Don't tell me you've forgotten what an alley looks like in two short years."

Astonishment warred with absurd laughter. "You got us from the town steps into an alley barely wide enough for two bodies, and I didn't feel it?"

He nibbled her jaw. "Pretty sure we both felt plenty of things, angel, just nothing as insignificant as lateral motion."

With a sound between a laugh and a groan, she dropped her head onto his shoulder. "This is so out of context, Aidan. There's a murderer running around the Cove. He shot George, kidnapped Steven and could have seriously hurt an old man. We're fairly certain his boss is en route to kill me and possibly you, as well. So what do we do? We come this close to having sex in an alley. We're sick."

"We're human."

"We'll be human corpses if we're not careful."

"Demars will have to go through me to get to you."

"That does not make me feel better." When his eyes glinted again, she drew back so fast she rapped her head against the stone wall behind her. "Ouch. No, don't," she warned.

"I was only going to kiss you." His lips twitched. "No need to give yourself a concussion."

"Been there, done that, not anxious to repeat." Using the flat of her hand, she held him off. "Steven's philosophy when he taught my cousin Addie and me to kickbox was that we'd never learn if we didn't do any full-contact sparring."

"He used full contact on nine-year-old girls?" The

glint deepened to a threat. "I should leave him to Weasel for that."

"He knocked us down hard on two separate occasions. The third time we decided to hell with fair play and kicked him in the crotch. He's my cousin, he kept your secret, and I want a chance to kick him there again for doing that."

"Jesus, Raven, your family and men's genitalia do not get along."

Her eyes danced as she closed fingers on the front of his jeans. Easing forward, she stopped her mouth half an inch from his and let a satisfied smile tilt her lips. "Liar."

With very fortunate timing, she suspected, her phone rang.

"Saved by the bell." But he caught her mouth briefly anyway and made her vision blur.

When it cleared, she saw a muscle in his jaw twitch. Why was news never good, she wondered, and turned the phone to see? The screen read: Steven. The text message read: Three feathers from a raven means death in this town. Your cousin has two…and the barrel of my gun pressed to his head.

THE MAN CALLED WEASEL tossed his prisoner's phone onto a stone slab.

"That's a prime piece of junk you got there, pal. Johnny Demars, he made it a policy a long time ago that his employers would always have state-of-the-art equipment. Pay's not bad, either."

"Yeah? Ask him if he needs a good lawyer next time you see him."

Snorting, Weasel took a drink from the Mason jar he'd filched from the campsite. Slices of fruit bobbed in a colorless liquid that had burned like hellfire with the first few sips. But after a while, it just kind of slid on down like honey.

Curious, he snagged a pear. "You can ask for yourself." A wide smile split his face. "If you've got the nerve."

"Does that mean I'm going to meet Johnny Demars?"

"Only in writing." The fruit was fine, the drink far better. "Way I figure it, no one should ever *want* to see JD. Kind of like you don't want to look at that woman with snakes for hair."

"Medusa."

"One turns you to stone, the other turns to dust. Now me, I got plans for the future, big plans. But until the day I can make 'em happen—coming soon, Cousin Blume—I do what I'm told to do on my state-of-the-art smartphone, and I don't go looking for faces that'd rather not be seen."

"Sounds reasonable."

"I'm a reasonable guy. Smart, too. Got a brand-new watch and some extra bills to prove it. Man, your great-granddaddy's older than the land I'm standing on."

"It's a close call."

A lopsided smile appeared. "He's old, and your cousin's hot. I mean, she is smokin'."

"I'm sure her husband would agree."

Weasel sneered. "He's not so much. Won't be anything at all when this is over."

"Is that when we all die?"

"If that's what the writing says, yep. Meanwhile, the lady's a looker and I got a yen for black hair and go-on-forever legs. Your cousin, she could wrap a man like me up for a good long time."

"Long enough for her husband to put a bullet in your head."

Weasel smirked. "You're overestimating him and underestimating me."

"Always possible. But how do you think Mr. Demars would react to you getting yourself 'wrapped up,' so to speak, with the woman he plans to kill?"

"Don't have to think. What JD doesn't know can't hurt me, simple as that."

"If you say so."

"I do." Standing, Weasel gave the ground a minute to settle. "I do, and I'm *gonna* do whatever the hell I want until the boss gets here. Maybe after, too"

He made a circle with the tip of his gun. "Now you stay put, Cousin Blume, and don't go waking the neighbors. No sense you dying before your time."

"I'll put the party on hold until you get back."

"You do that." Smiling hugely, Weasel placed the carving knife he habitually carried next to the Mason jar. Then he set his sights on the door, and his mind on dark-haired Raven Blume. Demars had told him under no circumstances to kill her. But there'd been no mention of him not having a little Weasel fun.

Chapter Nine

By midafternoon, Raven counted over a hundred tents and camper vans scattered about the clearing and half again that many people occupying them.

A collection of market stalls had sprung up next to the site. Canopied tables, vendor pickups and even blankets spread out on the grass were stocked with merchandise. The wares ranged from sunhats and sandals to artwork and jewelry to T-shirts and handmade soaps. At least six of the sellers also carried incense.

"People are burning sticks of jasmine and hyacinth everywhere we go." Her smile teased the man at her side. "I suppose it is marginally possible that Weasel's here." The tease spread to her eyes. "Alone in the crowd."

"Laughing on the inside, Raven." Aidan's assessing gaze didn't miss a beat, but she saw the corners of his mouth turn up.

The question she'd started to ask in town came back to her as a couple forking up egg foo yong with chopsticks strolled past.

"If not Weasel, Aidan, who do you think spent the night in the vacant apartment?"

"Same person as you, I imagine."

"Fergus?"

"Guy likes clean bathrooms."

"Why didn't you tell Emma?"

He moved a shoulder. "Minor break and enter aside, his reasons for being in Raven's Cove appear relatively altruistic"

She eyed his unrevealing profile. "Why do you say 'appear'? Don't you believe his story?"

"Not until I clear it with Gaitor. I tried the last cell phone number I had for him. No luck."

"Wait, stop, reverse." Hooking his arm, Raven back-pedaled to admire a pair of glittery amethyst drop earrings.

"We also have to consider or at least acknowledge George's 'big guy' warning."

She drew her brows together. "If Demars is coming here himself, wouldn't two hit men be overkill?"

"Or insurance."

"I thought that's what kidnapping Steven was supposed to be."

"Double indemnity."

"Overkill," she repeated, and picked up a pair of braided silver hoops. "As for Fergus being the 'big guy' in question, which I assume is what you were suggesting, my response to that is—Gaitor's nephew."

"So he says. I'll look online later, see if I can confirm his story."

She sighed. "Life is an enormous cesspool of spies and suspicious characters to you, isn't it?" Holding the hoops up to her ears, Raven regarded her reflection in a small display mirror. "I would truly hate to be a cop." Unsure, she tipped her head to the side. "What do you think?"

Even as she asked the question, she spotted the man behind her. He met her eyes in the mirror, but reacted so swiftly to the visual contact that by the time she spun to look, he'd vanished.

"Did you see—well, no you wouldn't have." She pointed. "Just for a second, Aidan, there was a man in front of that blue tent. He had a thin face, close-set eyes, and scruffy brown hair. Like a weasel."

"Which way did he go?"

"To his left, our right." Impatience rose. "I know I saw him. Am I being paranoid?"

"Killer," Aidan reminded, and, taking her hand, drew her along the vendors' row. "Let's do it this way. First we'll blend and skulk. Later, if necessary, we'll eavesdrop. Here, try this on." Snagging a bush hat from a long table, he placed it on her head.

She pushed the brim up. "It's a little big, isn't it?"

"Makes it perfect." After paying, he dropped his sunglasses down and draped an arm over her shoulders. "So. You hungry?"

"I had a lemon square at Rooney's, and you gave me soggy cereal for breakfast. What do you think?"

"That you'll want something more substantial for lunch."

"I take it we're not going Weasel hunting."

"If he's watching us, he'll surface again."

"Wasn't it you who said that if one of Demars's men was watching us, we wouldn't see him?"

"Maybe Weasel didn't get the memo."

"Or he wanted us to see him."

"Or that."

"Any other possibilities before I settle down to only worrying about those particular two? Oh, wait, I forgot, Weasel won't try anything as long as we're in a crowd."

"Pretty sure I never said that, angel. Come on, let's eat."

He steered her toward a sleek silver catering truck that boasted an efficient drop-down side. Behind the counter, a dark-haired woman with lines bracketing her mouth cut sandwiches into quarters and sang along with the Beatles on her iPod.

"I don't know any raven-related songs," she confessed. "But I can offer you raven burgers—that would be the usual beef covered with black sauce—raven dogs—same sauce—raven egg salad sandwiches—not the genuine article—and of course, ravenberry juice to wash any or all of those things down."

"Hang on a minute." A large, barrel-chested man with sandy-red hair and singed oven mitts hastened over. "You folks are missing the boat. Literally. I've got every kind of fish you can name at my truck. This place is flash, but mine's the real gem." He winked broadly at Raven. "Your companion looks like a mussel man to me."

The woman gave her fingers a dismissive flip. "Go away, Hector."

"Herron."

"Whatever. Go bad-mouth the guy who's selling black cotton candy. Or better yet, that preacher who scared off the early lunch crowd."

Aidan regarded the rotisserie. "We'll try the dogs. What did the preacher do?"

"He didn't have to do anything." The woman snapped on a pair of latex gloves and picked up a bun before opening the oven door. "Loony like that only has to hang around and stare." She shook her tongs in Raven's direction. "If I had your face, hon, I'd keep a weather eye out for him. He'll stare the clothes right off your body."

"Over my dead one." Aidan paid while Raven bit it. "Any idea where he is now?"

"Not here, thank the Lord. It's five for the dogs. Another two, and I'll throw in a quart of juice. It's a good deal," she told the red-haired man who merely snorted and sidled closer to Raven.

"You come see me at dinnertime, pretty lady. I've got a fresh Maine lobster with your name written all over it."

"Sounds—"

The word *delicious* never made it out. With a quick "Let's go," Aidan twirled her around and pushed.

"What?" she demanded.

"Man. Between those booths."

She glimpsed a black figure, then nothing but shadows. "Was it Weasel?"

"Nope. This guy had a beard, glasses and a bigger hat than yours. My bet's on Reverend Alley."

She had to jog to keep up. "You're wasting your time. Alley's too much of a caricature to be Johnny Demars. Besides, he's been here since yesterday, and if killing me was his goal, he had the perfect opportunity outside Two Toes Joe's bar last night."

"We might be able to cut him off. Lose the food."

Raven swallowed the growl in her throat along with a final bite of dog. "At this rate, I'll die of starvation before Demars gets anywhere near me." Ditching the remainder in a plastic bin, she wiped her fingers and surveyed the gap between the booths. "He's not here, Aidan."

"No, he's there."

She followed his gaze and spotted the reverend hastening toward a dense section of woods.

"Come on."

She had no trouble keeping pace—until they reached the sleeping tents, and more people appeared to impede their progress.

What little sun had struggled through the clouds earlier in the day was gone. Not a breath of air stirred the overhead branches. No insects buzzed or hummed, no leaves rustled. It was—unearthly, Raven decided. Very much the calm before the storm.

Like a herd of animals sensing a predator, the campers moved in restless patterns. Until a single gunshot fired in the vicinity of the previous night's campfire turned restless movement into a stampede.

One man, his gaze trained skyward, bounced off another man's chest and into Raven's arm. A larger, sullen-looking man deliberately blocked their path. When Aidan grabbed him by the jacket and threw him aside, he took two wobbly steps and crashed into a pup tent. The frame collapsed, the occupant screamed, and the man was promptly jumped by a pair of angry females.

"My arm's broken," he shouted. "Stop hitting me!"

Slowing, Raven looked back. There were three women now, pummeling the guy with their fists. Under the canvas, the trapped occupant continued to scream. No longer able to see Aidan through the sea of gathering bodies, she debated for a moment, then detoured toward the collapsed tent to help.

That was the plan, anyway.

She was wading into the crowd when a hand clamped on to her arm and yanked her roughly around.

"Hey there, lovebird, you looking for me?"

She spied close-set eyes, thin features and a shock of brown hair before the man spun her away from him. His surprisingly strong hand snicked her arm up behind her back. With the other, he jabbed a gun into the right side of her spine. His mouth moved against her temple.

"Turn left, walk, don't make a sound, don't move a wrong muscle. I can hurt you plenty and not kill you."

She hitched in a breath as he twisted harder on her arm.

"Very good, Raven," he congratulated. "Now smile

and cross your fingers that the people we pass keep right on going. Else we'll be navigating a field of corpses to reach our love nest."

FOR THE MOST PART, Aidan kept Reverend Alley in sight. Focusing his eyes forward, he called back to Raven. "We should be able to intercept him. Stay close."

The undergrowth had thickened substantially. Wild bushes topped seven feet and the ground grew rougher with every step. Weed-choked gullies appeared to his left, a high wall of rock to his right.

Ten yards ahead, the reverend splashed through a small creek. He was laboring visibly, Aidan realized. He would have called out if the man hadn't tripped and plowed into the trunk of an evergreen. Alley avoided a head-on collision, but in doing so caught his toe on an exposed root and wound up staggering in a drunken circle.

He threw his hands up when he saw the hit coming. Because of that, Aidan was able to catch him around the middle, flip both of them in the air and land with his captive on top of, rather than underneath, him. Which would have been fine if he hadn't also banged his own head on a log and ended up seeing stars. Next time, he thought hazily, he was going to call out.

"Got what you deserved, didn't you, for trying to knock an old man senseless."

A smug voice floated down to him. Using his hands to push, Aidan rolled the reverend off and got to his knees. "You're heavier than you look," he muttered, rubbing his head.

"You should've had me before I reached the creek." Hampered by his long coat, the reverend climbed awkwardly to his feet, steadied himself, then let a slow grin cross his face. "Dammit, McInnis, I always said you were a cat with nine lives."

As the last of the stars faded, Aidan stood to face him. "Hey, Gaitor. It's been a long time."

"Two years, three weeks and two days, you freaking mick." One huge bear hug and several backslaps later, Gaitor poked an accusing finger into his chest. "I'll lay eight to five odds that this was your lunatic idea, and Beckett was in on it up to his superior eyeballs."

"You needed to believe," Aidan said simply. With his breath back and his head clearing, he flicked a hand at Gaitor's beard. "Reverend Alley? Seriously? You actually dreamed this up?"

"You always said I had the sense of humor of a nerdy twelve-year-old."

"When you bother to display a sense of humor, you do." A brow went up. "You wanna tell me about Fergus?"

Gaitor chuckled. "What can I say? He's my sister's kid. Obviously, covert ops aren't his thing, but he has a willing heart."

When the bushes behind him shook, Aidan raised his voice. "Over here, Raven. I've got your red-eyed fanatic"

He glanced back as he spoke—and immediately felt an icy ball of terror surge up into his throat.

Staring at him, wide-eyed and confused, around the edge of a tall bush was a woman he'd never seen before.

WEASEL WALKED HER PAST—God, she lost track of the number—thirty or forty people, all rushing to see what was taking place at the tent site. Thankfully, none of them appeared to notice anything irregular.

He had the barrel of his gun lodged between her vertebrae and her arm yanked up so high, she couldn't believe it hadn't snapped at the elbow.

"You're doing real good, Raven. Once we run the food and junk gamut, we're home free. See how easy it is when I don't have to shoot a bunch of people along the way?"

"Where are we going?" The pain in her arm was so bad, Raven had to grind the question out between her teeth.

He lowered his mouth to her ear. "Five more minutes, lovebird, and you'll see."

She toughed it out. Had to. Move wrong or struggle, and he'd start shooting. Not her—that would be against orders—but anyone else unfortunate enough to be in the vicinity would be toast.

They circumvented the west wing rubble and headed for the north side of the house. He kicked open an iron gate grown wild with vines and creepers, then used his shoulder to close it. Lopsided headstones dotted a bushy plot of land. He located a path and jerked her onto it. With the greenery so high and widespread, she didn't spot the crypt until they rounded a sharp bend.

"Here's where the rotting dead come to rest and the sneaky living to hide. Say hello to your ancestors, Raven Blume."

Once inside, he released her with a shove that sent her sprawling to her hands and knees. Her eyes locked on a pair of scuffed boots and shot quickly up.

"Thank God." She exhaled in huge relief. "You're alive."

Steven, bound at the wrists to an iron wall ring, bared his teeth in a grimace. "Pleasure to see you, too, cousin." As Weasel started toward them, Steven mouthed, *Stand up fast and move.*

Without hesitation, she climbed to her feet, shook off a dizzy spell and eased away from her cousin.

Demars's smiling, practically salivating hit man

tracked her every step. "Time for you and me to have some fun, I think."

Terror wanted to choke her, but, like the dizziness, she fought it and continued to inch along the marble wall. "I can't imagine your employer would be very happy if you, uh, messed me up before he arrived."

"I'm not gonna mess you up, lovebird. We're just gonna have a little fun is all."

Steven made a subtle head motion to keep her going. Stall, she thought, and latched onto the first thing that crossed her mind. "You fired that shot back at the campsite, didn't you?"

"Works every time. Folks scatter like magpies. Some of them get rude. A few get downright mean. And there you have it, instant chaos." He ran his tongue over front teeth that jutted from his mouth at a comical angle. "What kind of bra you wearing under that tight shirt?"

Panic spurted, but she battled past it. "You're getting a little ahead of yourself, aren't you?"

"Can't have any fun if you keep your clothes on."

"Okay." She made herself hold Weasel's stare. "But in that case, we should probably have a drink first, don't you think? I mean, it's not really fair, is it? You're all— well, lets say you're nicely loosened up, and I haven't had a drop of anything since last night."

Licking his teeth again, he glanced at the Mason jar on the stone slab. "I guess I can spare a little if it'll keep your screams from breaking my eardrums." He wiggled his fingers. "I know how to hurt without leaving a mark. Can't let you go comatose, though." His eyes glittered. "Ain't no enjoyment in it for me when that happens."

She could do this, Raven thought, and worked to calm her scrambling heart. He was more than half cut already, and that home brew he'd stolen had a wicked finish.

"Thermos cup'll do you fine." Grabbing her head in passing, he gave her a kiss that almost made her gag.

"Please find me, Aidan," she prayed.

In the process of setting his gun on the slab, Weasel sent her a suspicious look. "What'd you say?"

"I said that stuff in the jar looks good." When he handed her a brimming plastic cup, she raised it quickly, before he could assault her mouth again. And dredged up a smile. "To your health," she said. Then without looking at Steven, added a silent, *And hopefully more to ours.*

HE COULDN'T FIND HER anywhere. Although panic churned inside, Aidan shoved the bulk of it into a mental box and twisted the lock. If he didn't shut it down, he couldn't help her. Better to use just the rough edges to keep his mind sharp and cycling through the possibilities.

"I might've seen her." The camper who'd given them the liquor last night scratched under his beard. "She was heading west with a skinny-assed guy. Seemed strange to me she'd leave, given the potential for injury when that tent collapsed. She's a doctor, right? Fellow I met said he thought she was a doctor."

Tension coiled in Aidan's belly. Weasel had her. But he'd already figured that, hadn't he, when he'd realized that the wrong woman had followed him from the campsite.

He scanned the grounds ahead. Where would the bastard take her?

The tents had limited potential. Too many of them looked too much alike, making it all too easy for anyone to wander through a wrong flap.

He considered Blume House, but nixed that idea as well. Too high profile. Plus, Weasel wasn't familiar with the place. Even with Steven out of the picture, the risk of discovery outweighed the safety factor.

An outbuilding then, one not readily visible to curious eyes.

As he approached the market, Aidan slowed from a run to a jog. He tried to recall how many freestanding structures he'd noticed in the past two years. The number had to be upward of twenty, so he could probably double that to include the secreted ones.

"Lose your partner, did you?" The man who'd been pushing mussels on Raven earlier flapped a pot holder from behind his grill. "Remind her I've got a delicious lobster dinner waiting for her tonight."

"Move your damn grill to another spot, fish man," the dark-haired woman shouted from her catering truck. "You're suffocating me and my customers with your smoke."

Tuning them out, Aidan ran through the dwindling list of prospects.

Instinct drew him to the ruined west wing. When he spied a movement in one of the shadows, he snapped the gun from his waistband.

Not Raven, he realized instantly. But it was someone he'd seen before. And she was waving her arms as she ran toward him.

"You're the doctor's friend, aren't you?" Gulping air, a woman with short blond hair and a cut on her cheek stumbled to a halt. "I was sitting over there, reading about the house and the evil, and I saw her come by with a man—a creepy man. He had a gun stuck in her back. I knew he hadn't seen me, so I waited, then I followed them. Your lady helped me last night when I was a drunk and acting weird. It's my turn to help her back." She took hold of his wrist. "Come with me."

Chapter Ten

"You surely can hold your liquor, lovebird." Weasel gave a sloppy wink. "It takes a woman with balls to do that."

Not the most flattering description, Raven reflected, but he was slurring his words quite badly now, and that was a promising sign.

She deliberately kept her distance from Steven. Whatever he was doing involved a great deal of covert arm and shoulder movement, as well as the odd grimace of pain.

With his gait off-kilter, Weasel tossed back the last of the alcohol in the Mason jar. Please be enough, Raven prayed. She struggled not to recoil when he walked up to her and, face-to-face, hung his left arm over her right shoulder. "Fight me," he ordered.

Her stomach clutched. "Um, now? Before I'm finished…?"

The plastic cup flew from her fingers. Showing his prominent front teeth, Weasel grabbed her shoulders. "You fight me, Raven Blume, else I'm gonna start hurting parts of you you'd rather I didn't."

He'd do that anyway, she realized, until she screamed. Then he'd do more until those screams got him off.

Her throat muscles didn't want to work. She had to beat back the panic that controlled them.

"Do you want it clean or dirty?" she managed to ask.

His bloodshot eyes lit up even as his hands slid downward to grip her arms. "Surprise me."

Closing her own eyes briefly, she sucked in a mental breath and moved to knee him. As expected, he laughed and blocked the blow, leaving her free to slam her fist into his ear.

When he howled, she shoved him backward. Remember the lessons, she told herself, and used her foot to side kick his knee low and his torso high.

He stumbled into a wall still howling—and, unfortunately, still smiling. Sort of. The expression on his face had changed to one of excitement tinged with anger.

"Bitch," he swore. But he made a come-ahead motion with the fingers of both hands. "You hurt me good there, lovebird. Now I want you to take your very best shot. You get one more freebie."

Without hesitation, she went for a hook kick to the head.

The surprise on his face told her he hadn't seen it coming, but he got a hand up fast and tried to trap her ankle.

His bleary eyes flashed with something ugly when he missed. "My turn now," he warned. He took a single pawing step and charged.

Raven knew he was going to ram her into the wall. She ducked to her right, saw him correct and braced for the blow. However, instead of being butted against marble, she was mowed down from the side by Steven's flying body.

Weasel cursed, her cousin snarled and the two men grappled briefly on the floor. Steven got in three solid punches before Weasel nailed him in the throat, did a shoulder roll and yanked a gun from his boot.

"Twitch, either of you, and I'll put a bullet between

Cousin Blume's eyebrow rings." Staring Steven down, he aimed a finger at Raven. "You, over here!"

She'd made it halfway to the slab where Weasel's larger gun sat. When he barked at her, she halted and drew her outstretched hand back. She should have gone for the knife lying next to Steven's ropes.

"I'll give you credit for jumping on an opportunity I was dumb enough to give you, Blume, but you put one foot wrong, and your party's history...I said, over here," he shouted at Raven. "Party—history," he reminded, and put pressure on the trigger.

She did as she was told, and only shuddered once when he dragged her up against him, thankfully with her back to his front.

Teeth gritted, he waved his gun in Steven's face. "I can carve you into pieces, no problem. Or—damn, no, I can't. If I do that, there won't be a hostage like the big D wanted." He snugged his arm under Raven's breasts, swayed slightly and appeared torn. "What to do here, lovebird, what to—"

She felt the reaction of his muscles before she understood the reason for it. It wasn't until she saw blood spurt from his shoulder and heard him swear that she realized he'd been shot.

His gun struck the floor with a clatter. He made a choking sound as a bloody river ran along his forearm.

"Let her go, Weasel."

Aidan...

Raven's eyes combed the shadows—and found him in the darkness next to one of the lesser tombs.

"You've got three seconds before I put a bullet in your skull, pal. Two, one..."

Weasel flexed his biceps, but it was an instinctive reaction. Whipping his arm free, he sent Raven stumbling over Steven into Aidan, then ran from the crypt.

Steven bit off a yell when her foot landed between his legs. Fortunately, Aidan caught her before she smashed into the tomb.

Setting her upright, he pushed the hair from her face with his fingers and stared into her eyes. "Are you hurt?"

"What? No. God, you're here." She grabbed hold, hugged him and fisted his shirt. "I knew you'd come. No, I'm not hurt."

He kissed her once, hard, then again before releasing her to kick Weasel's gun in her direction. "Stay here, stay together," he said. "He'll have a backup weapon, and he won't hesitate to use it."

"No, wait, I think…" But Raven was already talking to herself. "This is his backup," she ended on a growl.

Glowering, Steven crawled to his feet. "Your aim's pathetic, Raven. You got the creep in the knee and almost made a eunuch out of me. You're welcome, by the way."

Her response was interrupted by a scream from outside. A single, high-pitched shriek followed by a series of short, whimpering bursts.

Raven's heart actually stopped beating. "He's killed Aidan," she breathed.

Ongoing whimpers led her, weak-kneed, through the tangled foliage to a collection of crumbling headstones.

She spotted Aidan on his feet and released her breath in a rush.

He stood near one of the markers, staring at the ground. Several yards behind him, the blonde woman from Joe's bar held her arms in an X across her chest. Her mouth was open, and her eyes were huge with fright.

"What happened?" Steven demanded.

But Raven saw the skinny, unmoving legs and knew. Weasel was dead.

Aidan held out a hand to her.

She'd seen death before, but never like this. The bullet had entered through the hit man's throat, blown his Adam's apple wide open and likely exited through his neck.

"Was it you?" she asked, but the sideways look Aidan sent her killed that hopeful thought.

She leaned against him, suddenly exhausted. "I wanted it to be you who got him. I'm sorry, but I did."

"I wanted it to be me," her cousin remarked. Then he shrugged. "He's dead, though, so I'm good."

Running a hand along Raven's arm, Aidan shook his head, "You're missing the point, Steven."

"Why? There was nothing he could have told you. He never met or even saw Johnny Demars."

"Still not the point."

"In your own time then, Aidan."

Raven stared at Weasel's face, at his protruding teeth and glassy, unblinking eyes. "Think about it," she said softly. "If Aidan didn't do this, who did? That's the point, Steven. Weasel's death means Johnny Demars is here in Raven's Cove."

AIDAN DEALT WITH THE CORPSE while Raven and her cousin did what they could to calm down the blond woman whose name was Sylvie. A handful of oblivious people passed them near the woods, but by then they'd reached the west wing and were safely out of sight of the crypt.

Steven steered Sylvie toward the tent grounds. "I'll convince her to keep this to herself," he promised.

"Yeah, really good luck with that," Raven murmured in his wake.

"Talking to yourself could be construed as a sign of inherited ancestral tendencies," a familiar voice remarked.

"Gaitor?" Whirling, she spotted the bearded reverend and ran to hug him. Tightly. "You," she punched his shoulder, "are a major rat."

"I need to stay in character," he whispered and, separating himself, gave her a solemn once-over. "You look beautiful, Raven, as always."

"I look like death—which it just so happens, I've seen far too much of lately."

"Another bad sign. Fall into step with the crazy man, and fill me in."

The news about George in particular hit him hard. They found a log near the woods and sat down.

"I'm really sorry, Gaitor," Raven said gently.

"I wouldn't have expected one of our own to turn like that."

"Me, neither." She patted his leg. "I don't think Aidan was as surprised, though."

"I'm not so much surprised as I am disappointed, and pissed that I never considered the possibility." When he raised a palm to a woman with a long black braid, a trace of humor entered his tone. "Poor Trisha. She got swept up in the melee that unfolded here and found herself running after Aidan who was running after me."

"No one should have been running in the first place." The pat became a rap on Gaitor's knee. But she grinned. "He thought she was me, didn't he?"

"Yep. When he saw she wasn't, he flew back to the clearing so fast you were probably found and free by the time I made it out of the woods."

"Fergus said you've been keeping an eye on me since Aidan's funeral. He also said you were following a lead on Demars, and that's why he—Fergus—trailed me to Maine."

"Yes, well that's not quite true, though in fairness to Fergus, it's the story I gave him."

"Okay. What's the real story?"

"I haven't let you out of my sight since Aidan—damn the crafty bastard—'died.' Don't get me wrong, I fully understand why he did it."

"Yes, we've been through the eye-for-an-eye thing."

"He wanted you safe, Raven."

"Been through that, too."

"There you go, then. Aidan and me both did what we thought was best. Still, even with him gone, I couldn't get it out of my head that Demars might decide to off you, just for the hell of it. Time passed, and nothing happened. But every once in a while I'd see someone who looked to be watching you, and my first thought would always be Demars."

"No wonder I felt like a bug under a microscope. But, Gaitor, if you knew I was coming to Raven's Cove and you intended to be here yourself, why did you need Fergus to come, as well?"

"I wanted someone closer to you than I, in my ministerial disguise, could get."

She smiled. "Are you saying Fergus doesn't know you're really Uncle Alley Gaitor?"

"No—and don't give me that look."

"What, like I haven't met your weird sense of humor before today?" As her tension subsided, Raven massaged the knotted muscles in her neck. "This has been one truly bizarre experience."

"I hate to sound gloomy, but I feel it necessary to point out that in no way is this nightmare remotely close to over. Truth be told, my gut says hell's about to break loose in this spooky little section of Maine."

"Hell and Ravenspell," she agreed. As if summoned, three ravens glided in for a landing, two on a tent to her right and one on the ground in front of her. "If three feathers mean death," she mused, "what might three live ravens portend?"

"It could mean that evil's closing ranks," a voice behind her remarked.

Laughing, Raven poked an elbow into Aidan's ribs. "You're so cynical, you'd make the same prediction about three turtledoves."

"Song says two turtledoves, but forget the birds. What we've got here are two corpses and still very little to go on in terms of Johnny Demars."

"We know he's in the Cove." Raven seesawed her head. "But that's not exactly positive knowledge, is it?"

Gaitor shrugged with his mouth. "As trite as it sounds—forewarned, forearmed. And unless Demars has telepathic powers, I might yet, in my fanatical guise, be considered the ace up our collective sleeve."

Leaning over, Raven gave his cheek a peck. "You're an ace at clichés, anyway. Thank you, Gaitor, for everything."

"You want to thank your ace properly, slip him a bottle of whiskey. Are you sure, both of you, that Weasel didn't offer up anything useful about Demars?"

"Not to me or Steven," Raven said. "However…" Reaching back, she grabbed a handful of Aidan's too-long hair and pulled him forward. "See that cryptic half smile? That's the kind of smile a perceptive woman can feel on her skin. Means there's something he hasn't told us."

"And won't if you rip my hair out."

"Girl," she accused.

"Bully," he countered.

"Pax, people." Gaitor held up a hand. "Plans to make here, deaths to thwart."

Raven gave Aidan's hair an amused last tug before releasing him. "He started it."

Grinning, he lifted her off the log, sat and settled her on his lap. "Just how do you figure that, angel?"

Eyes twinkling, she kissed his jaw. "You got my stolen laptop back."

"Got your new hat back, too, along with Rooney's watch and cash. Do I get extra brownie points for any of that?"

"Only if you tell us what is it you know that we don't?"

He dropped the bush hat on her head. "After I put Weasel's body in the crypt I took a look around and discovered a stashed backpack with a mini cassette recorder inside."

"Cassette, as in tape?"

"You sound surprised."

"I am, a little. Steven said that Weasel said that every piece of equipment Demars and his people own and or use is state-of-the-art."

"With one exception, it appears." Reaching into a black canvas pack behind him, Aidan retrieved the device.

Raven tilted her head at it. "Are there tapes?"

"One. It's inside."

"And of course you've listened to it."

"I mentioned eavesdropping earlier, right? Play it now, and we'll compare notes."

Although she wasn't sure she wanted to, Raven pressed the button.

A long hiss preceded a click, followed by a young man's voice.

"I can do what I want to now. There's no one left to stop me."

There was a protracted pause, then a more agitated, "You made this happen. Everything was fine. We were how a family's supposed to be. But you wanted things to be different, so you made sure they changed."

After another lengthy pause, his tone grew heated.

"You told me you hated death, but I don't think you do. I'll keep your stupid secret, but you'll never measure up. And neither will I from now on."

Raven heard a faint rasp of sound and a second click. Then a man's deeper voice said simply, "Jason...."

Chapter Eleven

She'd come to Raven's Cove prepared to open a clinic at Blume House. Now there were dead people hidden on the property, a former cop masquerading as a fanatical reverend, and a faceless crime lord killer lurking in the shadows. Thanks to Weasel, they might have a snippet of Johnny Demars's voice, but as clues went, Raven didn't think it was much.

From the grass near the woods, she watched another vanload of people bump their way onto the site. "We should do what Riese did and rent out rooms at the house. We'd make a fortune. If Demars turned out to be one of the guests, maybe the evil that inhabits the walls would infect him."

"It's more likely Demars would infect the walls." Sitting on the step up to Reverend Alley's Romany-style RV, Aidan replayed Weasel's cassette tape. "Gaitor wants to stay there tonight."

"Does he know about the walls?" Raven continued to sift through the hit man's belongings. So far she'd unearthed seven gleaming knives and two boxes of ammo. "This guy was seriously sick. The carving knife Steven used to cut his ropes was so sharp it slashed his wrists. I had to put four stitches in each of five lacerations." After which she'd splinted a fractured arm, wrapped a sprained ankle and treated a poked eye. "I've also been thinking about the kid we heard on the tape," she continued. "If it was Jason having a phone conversation—more than likely—he sounded like a very troubled adolescent."

"He sounded angry as hell."

"The way a kid might sound if he thought his father had engineered his mother's death."

"Murder's quicker than divorce."

"Thanks, but I'll take the papers. Do you think Demars killed her?"

"I don't know. The kid was definitely upset."

Raven reached into Weasel's backpack. "Upset is a state of mind for an adolescent. It's like a rite of passage. Except in Jason's case, he didn't pass so much as detour down a rockier path... Oh, yuck, men's boxers."

A faint smile touched Aidan's lips. "That's an awfully puritanical reaction for a physician, Raven."

"Fine, let's switch jobs. I'm sure there are plenty of other disgusting things in here." Warier now, she peered inside before she pulled anything else from the pack. "I'd rather Gaitor stayed with Rooney."

The smile that reached up into Aidan's dark eyes excited a rather lovely jitter in her stomach. "I must have missed the segue from Weasel's boxers to your great-grandfather."

"You'd have to be in my head—which you wouldn't want to be right now—to understand. My thoughts are bouncing around like a rubber ball. Suffice to say after everything that's happened today, I'm worried about Rooney. Steven will be there, but someone else should stay at the cottage as well. I called Grandpa's cell phone while you and Gaitor were plotting your cop strategy. He flatly refuses to go and visit my aunt Vera in Bangor during Ravenspell."

With his forearms resting on his knees, Aidan hit Play again. "What about Fergus?"

"Why would he want to visit Aunt Vera?" She smiled when his eyes came up. "Kidding. I thought maybe Fergus had gone AWOL now that his cover's been blown. Did he admit to the break and enter at Emma's apartment?"

"To me, yeah. Gaitor doesn't need to know."

"You can extend the omission to Rooney. By the end of Ravenspell, it'll be a man-size raven who did the deed. Okay, so that puts Fergus and Steven at the cottage and you, me and Gaitor at Blume House."

"No, that puts Gaitor at Blume House, and you and me here."

She stared. "You want us to hide in a tent? With heavy rain threatening, no locks on the flap and, oh yes, Johnny Demars out for blood?"

"I was thinking more along the lines of Gaitor's RV, but if you prefer to sleep on the ground, I'm game."

"This from the police lieutenant who spent six, no sorry, seven undercover nights sleeping in a gross Milwaukee warehouse in the middle of July, and whose face I barely recognized when he walked through the door, unshaved, unshowered and under the ridiculous impression that I'd be so deliriously happy to see him that I'd be willing to make out on the kitchen floor, pre-cleanup."

"It was the hall floor, Raven. We didn't make it to the kitchen."

"We did eventually." She used a magazine from Weasel's pack to fan her suddenly warm cheeks. "I think this conversation derailed somewhere along the line."

Setting the recorder inside the RV, Aidan stood and started across the grass toward her. "I wouldn't say that. Hard ground, hard surface." Reaching down, he snagged her hand and with an easy tug brought her to her feet. A smile grazed his lips. His eyes held steady on her face. "You might want to consider the wisdom of waving that porn magazine in my face."

Porn?

She glanced at the nearly naked cover model and couldn't suppress a laugh. "My God, how is any of this even happening? I'm trying to talk myself out of jumping you in the middle of a campsite—a setting that's a thousand times crazier than our kitchen, okay, hall floor, and instead of diffusing the situation, I whip out a red flag and wave it at a hot, Black Irish bull."

On the water beyond the high ridge, a low peal of thunder rumbled through the evening sky.

"Lose the magazine, Raven," Aidan said, and curled his fingers around her neck.

It was July in Milwaukee all over again, she realized. It was heat and hunger, deprivation and desire, tangling together and making the rest of the world melt away.

More thunder sounded in the distance. She sensed motion, caught a few murmuring voices, but all she really heard right then was the blood pounding like a war drum in her ears.

An almost uncontrollable urge to press herself against him, center to center, swept through her. She wanted to feel his arousal, and know that, like her, he was skating on the edge of his control.

True, no one directed that control better than Aidan, but no one lost it better, either. He could snatch the ground out from under her long before her mind caught up. Didn't matter though, because he'd be right there to catch her and take her to that place where sensation ruled and everything else was just a hazy detail.

With a smile blossoming and her body already reacting, Raven let the magazine flutter to the grass. "You know this isn't Milwaukee, right? Not a floor in sight." She hooked her fingers in his waistband, brought her mouth temptingly close to his. "Tell me Gaitor's already packed and gone, Aidan. Lie to me, if you're sure he won't be back for an hour or more. I want to know we'll have time to…" Leaving the rest to his imagination, she caught his lower lip between her teeth and simply savored the taste of him.

The fingers around her neck tightened. The gleam in his eyes deepened. "Does this mean you've gotten to wherever it is you need to be so we can have sex?"

She rubbed her hips against his jeans. "Why, Lieutenant McInnis, you put that so sweetly. So like a man. We're apart for a few short years, you reappear out of the blue, and suddenly it's all about sex. Call me a romantic prude—" she teased him with a kiss to the side of his ear "—but I prefer to think we'll be making love."

The last word was nothing more than a smothered syllable as he covered her mouth with his and went straight for the heat.

Need spiked in every cell of Raven's body. Sliding her fingers up into his hair, she held on and let herself ride the fiery lust into the deeper emotional well that fed it.

She wanted him, desperately, but somewhere in her muddled mind, she knew that none of what she wanted could happen out here.

"Aidan…" Dragging her mouth free, she made herself breathe. "We can—but we can't. Not on the grass."

"Okay. In that case, Gaitor's packed and gone."

"For an hour, right?"

"Oh, for God's sake, you two, take it inside." Steven's dry comment was accompanied by a sharp rap of knuckles on the top of Raven's head. "In case you haven't noticed, there's a life-and-death drama playing out here. Not to mention dozens of people in the vicinity."

Aidan kept his eyes on Raven's face. "Not for long if they're smart. It's going to rain."

"Good. Maybe that'll cool you off. Hope so, because we've been summoned to Blume House for a ghostly retelling of both the Raven's and Soldier's tales. I have the guest list in my hand, and you're on it."

Plastering a genial smile on her lips, Raven swung to face him. "This was your brilliant idea, wasn't it?"

"Only the Blume House part. Rooney wanted to do it at Two Toes Joe's bar, and I'm not in the mood for green beer."

Aidan held Raven firmly in front of him—which both amused her and helped diminish some of her animosity toward Steven. "How many people?" he wanted to know.

"Twenty-eight—the precise number of bodies that can be squeezed around the banquet hall table."

"*Bodies* being the operative word." Aidan's gaze swept the area. "A gathering of Blumes is not a good idea at the moment."

Steven's smile was benign. "Yes, I mentioned that to Rooney, several times. Raven can tell you how effective my warning was."

Because fat raindrops were beginning to fall and Aidan was as recovered as he was likely to get, Raven began collecting Weasel's belongings. "Maybe we can make Grandpa see reason." Cinching the pack closed, she tossed it to her cousin. "Tomorrow's the night of the Reenactment, right?"

"Unfortunately."

"He can tell the tales then, set the mood for it. Is he at home?"

"Get serious. It's almost six o'clock. He'll be at Two Toes Joe's by now."

Raven pulled out her iPhone. "You should talk to him, Aidan. Stubborn cop to stubborn old man. What?" she said when he snorted out a laugh. "It could work."

"Yeah, and a good fairy might show up to transform Johnny Demars into a bird. Don't hold your breath on either count, Raven."

"Dialing," she said, and handed him her cell. "I'll take over if he becomes a wall. And it's a spirit, not a fairy."

Grinning, Aidan walked away.

She swung back to her cousin. "You know we should be discouraging Rooney's habitual drinking, don't you?"

"Joe's bar is his second home, Raven. He can still beat most of the locals at darts, and that's after he's had three or four mugs of *tea*." Steven waved irritably at a wasp. "FYI, Sylvie's cool about today. Freaked, but cool. Uh..." Pausing, he lowered his free arm. Weasel's back-pack slipped from his fingers.

Raven glanced back. "What is it?" Unsure, she frowned. "Steven?"

Still not moving, he dropped his gaze to his left shoulder. Something glistened on the front of his jacket. His face was pale when he brought his eyes back to hers. "I think I've been shot."

"IT WAS A WARNING," Aidan said four tense hours later. "A statement of what Demars can do and how effortlessly he can do it. Don't react to him, Raven," he cautioned when she folded her arms and glared through the windshield of Rooney's Jeep. "It's what he wants—to piss you off and terrify you at the same time. Give in to either, and you give him the upper hand."

She slanted him a dark look. "I kind of think he already has that, don't you?"

"Not as much as he thinks, no."

"Because we've got his voice? The name of his son, probably spoken by him? I think the odds are in Demars's favor, Aidan. He could have killed Steven."

"But he didn't. He also went for the younger, stronger target, rather than Rooney, who wouldn't have fared as well as your cousin. Think cat and mouse. That's the game Demars is playing."

"And apparently winning."

"Oh, I wouldn't say that. Demars can't have been happy to discover that a man he'd relied on for years could no longer be trusted to carry out a proper hit. Worse still, Johnny had to pull the trigger on Weasel himself."

"If he actually did pull it. What about your 'big guy' insurance policy?"

"I haven't forgotten him."

"But?"

"No but." He flipped the windshield wipers on high to combat the rain that fell in angled sheets from a pitch-black sky. "Our dead informant told Gaitor that one of Demars's preferred shooters was strictly a rifleman. We know he wasn't referring to Weasel, so that only leaves the big guy, and Weasel wasn't shot with a rifle."

"Did it occur to you that Demars might have more than two hit men?"

"Informant said he's gone with the favored two for a lot of years."

"Aidan, your informant's been dead for four of those years. However—" she held up her hands "—in the interest of positive thinking, I'm willing to accept your theory. There's no 'big guy' in Raven's Cove."

"At the risk of winding you up again, that's not quite what I said."

"Fine, whatever, I'm done. Like Weasel, Steven was shot with a 9 mm semiautomatic in order to frighten and anger me—and possibly because Demars wanted to get us back for the fact that Weasel had to be taken out. So here's how Steven and I arranged things. Steven, Rooney, Fergus and three burly local males will be sleeping at the cottage tonight. Gaitor and two equally burly fishermen will be up at Blume House and, as before, you and I will be in Gaitor's RV. When he wasn't swearing at me before the anesthetic kicked in, Steven told me that Rooney had five RV and trailer hookups installed after the last Ravenspell. Please tell me, because I wasn't paying attention earlier, that Gaitor nabbed one of them."

"He's a man of the cloth, Raven. Of course he's hooked up."

She grinned. "Okay, let's say Gaitor's disguise has more than one benefit and get back to the subject of death, because if by some miracle Demars doesn't kill me, I can pretty much guarantee Steven will." Tucking a leg up, she turned in her seat. "Should we leave Raven's Cove, Aidan? Just take off and make Demars come after us? I'd rather he shot at me than at members of my family."

"He's made his statement, Raven, and had his criminal version of fun. Games aren't his thing. He'll be loading up for real next time."

"Oh, well, that makes me feel much better." She glanced skyward as thunder shook the road beneath them. "Adding in the horror show sound effects—nightmare complete."

"You'll feel less threatened when we're inside, eating the pizza Emma gave me while you were busy with Steven."

"Did she give you two bottles of red wine, an elbow to the ribs and a big wink as well?"

"Along those lines, yeah."

"That's her trying to make a silk purse out of a sow's ear—which is totally disgusting, so forget I even said it. Good situation out of a bad one in any case."

A jagged bolt of lightning shot into the trees directly ahead of them. The fact that Aidan didn't appear to notice let alone react to it, had her studying his profile. "Nothing fazes you, does it? You might not like a thing, but you don't let it stop you from doing what needs to be done with as little fuss as possible."

"I have my moments. Had a big one today when I discovered that you'd been taken from the campsite."

"But you found me." Lashes lowered, she tipped her head in speculation. "Saved me." A smile curved her lips. "Even got my new hat back. I'd say that rates a big thank-you."

"Does that mean we're going to have sex—sorry—make love?"

"Night's long." Reaching out, she switched off the Jeep's engine. "Assuming we don't get shot or struck by lightning, we should have time for both."

He let the vehicle glide to a halt on the side of Ridge Road. "You know the brakes and steering stop working when the engine cuts out, right?"

"Yeah, I've heard that." Not taking her eyes from his, she undid her seat belt. Then she crossed her arms, grabbed the hem of her T-shirt and pulled it smoothly over her head. "I also know, Lieutenant, that you're a whiz when it comes to dealing with the unexpected."

Eyes glinting in the barely there light, he lifted her over the console so she straddled him with her knees. "This is gonna be tricky, angel."

"I know." Running her palms from his shoulders down his arms, she leaned in until her lips moved against his. "But it's also gonna be fun."

Chapter Twelve

What it was, Aidan thought, when his mind was actually capable of thought again, was a rocket ride into the kind of need he hadn't let himself experience for two painfully long years.

Green eyes sparkling, Raven pushed both him and the seat back, reached for his fly and tugged the zipper down. Her hands were magic on his skin, drawing him out and driving him to the limit of his restraint at the same time.

The tricky part should have been losing their clothes, but in his fevered state of mind, Aidan managed to miss that side of it. Raven's hot, hungry mouth fed on his. Her hands were everywhere, on his face, his chest, his ribs, his hips. Pulling, tugging, sliding, pleasing.

"It needs to be rough the first time." She bit his bottom lip. "It's been so long, it has to be hard and fast and wild."

He could give her that, he reflected—just as soon as his blood pressure throttled back from a volcanic storm to a mere storm of fire. However they did it, he wanted her on the same page as him.

"Might be better if we slowed this down a bit, angel."

Her smile had a wicked edge, like the light in her eyes. "Is slow what you want, or have you forgotten how to make out in a vehicle?"

"A guy never forgets that. I just thought after today you might need a moment to catch up. Guess I was wrong."

"Guess you were." She kissed him long and deep. So deep, his hands moved instinctively to grip her hips and lift.

Dragging her mouth from his, she let her eyes close, her head fall back and her body slide, hot and silky, onto him.

He felt the flash, like a thunderbolt in his system. Then the explosion ripped through him and into her.

This was it, a distant part of his mind realized. This was the reason he'd been willing to die. This was woman he'd been willing to die for. Two years ago in Milwaukee, and again here in Raven's Cove.

SHE'D FORGOTTEN, RAVEN thought through a dizzying haze, how incredible they'd been together. Or perhaps more correctly, her memories had dulled with time.

They weren't dull at the moment. Aidan whipped her into a frenzy of need that stole her breath and shot a thousand volts of current into her bloodstream. Everything pulsed. He was rock hard inside her, and yet, somehow, he managed to make a deliciously tortuous exploration of her throat, her shoulders, her breasts.

Shapes and motion fused and blurred. They made it to the RV, but no farther than that. The door clicked closed behind her back as he pushed her up against it. The clothes they'd tossed on came off again. Her white T flew into darkness. His black one joined it. She wriggled out of her jeans, pushed impatiently at his. And finally, skin to skin, his hands cupped and lifted her so she could wrap her legs around his hips.

They'd find a horizontal surface eventually, she supposed, but by the time they did, they'd either be too tired to move or dead.

Because she craved the taste of him, she caged his head in her hands and brought his lips up to hers. "You have a breast fixation, Aidan." She tugged on his hair to keep his head up, then dove in and took what she wanted from his mouth.

It was control torn to shreds and all boundaries knocked aside. Her heart was a giant fist pounding in her chest. She ran her palms over sleek skin and taut muscle, changed position and slid her tongue along his jaw.

"Do it," she murmured against his neck. "Make us both crazy."

He shifted her so their eyes met in the shadowy entrance. "We've been crazy since that first night in the alley."

Still pinned between him and the door, she set her mouth next to his ear. "In that case, Lieutenant, I want you to make me crazier than I already am, than I always am when I'm with you." She nipped his earlobe. "I want you to make me scream."

"My pleasure, angel."

With so much energy already streaming through her, Raven didn't think it would take much to bring about that scream.

Locking his eyes on hers, Aidan adjusted his hold on her hips. Then bracing her spine against the door, he slid his hand between her legs.

The unexpected force of her orgasm stunned her. Her body arched, her lashes swept down, and her mind went numb from the burst of heat that streaked through her limbs to her nerve ends.

The force of her own response robbed her of breath and brought a sharp gasp, but it didn't make her scream—

until he brought her fully down onto him, and she was wrapped around him, and need and hunger exploded through her system all at once.

Her nails bit into his shoulders, scraped over slick skin and raked along his arms. She screamed his name, then moaned it as he pumped more heat deep inside.

Aware but not aware, she let desire flood through her. His hands weren't rough, but they weren't gentle, either, so even when she thought there couldn't be more, there was.

The climax was a raw punch of power, a glorious gift that left her stunned and absolutely boneless. The best she could do, with no part of her brain left functioning, was slither down the inside of the door to the floor.

Too thunderstruck to move any further, Raven let the aftershocks of their incredible—no, off-the-scale—love-making ripple through her.

"That was…" A luxurious sigh finished the thought. With her eyes closed and her skin still alive with delicious tingles, she murmured, "You have the perfect body, Aidan."

"Not from where I'm lying."

She managed to smile. "I feel like I'm floating."

"Floating, drowning, dead, it all works."

He moved first, and brought her with him, so she was fully on top of him, and he had the floor beneath his back.

"You've lost weight," he said against her hair.

Raven held up her index and middle fingers. "Two pounds. That's sixteen measly ounces for each year you were gone, and since I'm not two feet tall, it's made absolutely no difference to my dress size." Unable to focus her mind, she let her hand drop. "Why are we talking about dresses?"

"No idea. I'm still working on remembering my name."

She nuzzled his shoulder. "As long as you remember mine, we're good. We're also on the floor. Again."

"You say that like it's a bad thing."

She lifted her head just far enough to see him. "There are such things as beds, you know."

"Beds are bonuses for us."

"Apparently."

"Look at it this way, Raven. We're inside, we're alone, and we have food and wine. Not a hit man or crime boss in sight."

"Mmm. Except the pizza and wine are out in the Jeep."

A glimmer appeared in his eyes. "I'll flip you to see who makes a dash through the rain to get them."

"Sounds fair."

She should have known better than to test his mental recovery powers. Or his physical ones, either, for that matter. He got his hands around her waist while she was trying to figure out which direction to roll and pinned her on her back beneath him, in less than a second.

"Well, one, two, three, go," she said with a laugh. "Guess I lost the toss."

He gave her a mind-melting kiss, then nudged her legs apart with his knee. "Depends how you define the word. In my dictionary, we've got a win-win going here. I take on the rain, you take on another round of hard surface sex."

"If I must, I must," she agreed. Having finally determined that none of the shadows were stairs in disguise, she shoved him up and away just far enough to switch their positions. On top of him now, with her palms pressed flat to his shoulders, she lowered her mouth slowly to his. "Let the win-win begin."

NOTHING IN the universe was as galling to Demars as waiting for the perfect opportunity to strike.

Raven Blume would be the first to go, that was absolute. Not only had her cop husband killed Jason, but now she was responsible for Weasel's premature demise.

Watching her die would help put things right. Watching Aidan McInnis watch her die would be even more rewarding. McInnis would suffer, and then he would join his lovely wife in death.

Revenge complete.

Of course the plan was simple enough on paper, but the timing and execution, those were stickier points. Too bad it couldn't happen now, because a noisy night was optimum for murder. Tomorrow would have to do, but no later than that. Nothing screwed a plan worse than procrastination.

Twelve years ago, a sliver of lingering sentiment had caused a death to be delayed. In the end, that delay had sent a once-obedient son down an emotionally charged path of self-destruction.

More than likely, Jason would have died some other way, eventually, but Aidan McInnis had taken the matter out of everyone's hands, and that could not be tolerated.

Demars had heard talk of a WWI soldier here in Raven's Cove. The "eye for an eye" expression had come up more than once. It was a description that fit the current situation to an eerie T. In this case, it would be a dead wife in exchange for a dead son.

Satisfied, if not entirely happy, the crime boss went eyeball to eyeball with a fat Maine lobster, smiled nastily and dropped it into a pot of boiling water.

CONSIDERING ITS SIZE, Gaitor's RV boasted more conveniences than Raven had anticipated. The bedroom had a closet, the bathroom a shower. There was a fully equipped kitchenette, and even a small fireplace in the living room.

Midnight had long since come and gone by the time she and Aidan got around to heating the pizza, opening the first of two wine bottles and switching on the electric flame. By then, Raven figured her body had combusted at least five, possibly six, times. A delicious feeling of lethargy flowed in her veins, because, well, because the lights were low, Louis Armstrong was crooning in the background and somewhere along the line, they'd made their way to the shower—which had naturally resulted in more combustion.

"I'm too wired to sleep," she said with a sigh, "and still too dazzled to think, so I guess all that leaves us is food and drink, the sound of the rain on the roof and an RV full of shadows."

"Not to mention the prospect of more sex." Aidan reached around her for the wine bottle. "When and if sensation returns to my lower body."

Thunder beyond the ridge underscored the mellow tones of Louis's cornet. Wearing one of Aidan's dark cotton shirts, Raven lay on her stomach in front of the fire, hugged a cushion and regarded the dancing flames. "I see faces in firelight," she told him. "My mother's sometimes, yours most times, and for the past two years now, a featureless reaperlike head, with two red eyes and really sharp teeth."

"If you see a live version of that anywhere, let me know, and I'll shoot it. Nightmare done."

Smiling a little, she swirled the robust wine around her glass. "You're so literal, Aidan."

"Cop," he pointed out, then grinned and, with his back propped against the sofa, looked into the flames with her. "I asked Gaitor about the red eyes you saw outside the bar. He had a pair of contact lenses made as part of his Ravenspell disguise."

She sipped, considered. "People believe, you know. In Hezekiah—in the whole 'Raven's Tale' for that matter. Only about a quarter of the people I've talked to also know about the convalescing soldier who murdered the man he thought had killed his brother. I find it interesting that the true story tends to get overlooked in favor of the legend. Even I didn't know about the soldier until Grandpa mentioned him yesterday."

Aidan played with her damp hair. "If you were looking to be fascinated, which scenario would you go for? That the dead deer you came across on the forest floor had been torn apart by a grizzly bear or Bigfoot?"

"Since all deer are Bambi to me, I refuse to picture such a gruesome occurrence, however, I get your point. Rooney says the Reenactment covers the entire spectrum, from evil comes, to evil winds up trapped in bird, to evil might or might not have been banished—said banishment depending on how you view Hezekiah's fate. Still, no matter which side you're on there, the legend maintains that some part of the original evil that possessed him managed to detach itself and push its way into the walls and grounds of Blume House. Soldier cracked open an emotional door, evil slipped inside and went to work on his grief."

"Sounds like a Goth version of Demars's story as it relates to Jason's death."

The shadows shifted, and for a moment firelight played across Aidan's features. He wore only his jeans, and the muscles of his chest made Raven think he was poised to strike like a panther. With a last sip of wine, she rose to set the bottle and glasses aside. Then, keeping her eyes fastened on his, she crawled slowly toward him. "Now you tell me something, Aidan. If tonight was your last night on earth, and you could have one final wish, what would it be?"

"I can tell you what it wouldn't be," he said as her fingers got busy on his fly. Keeping one knee raised, he supported her while she worked the zipper. "I wouldn't wish away the last two years of my life."

"Because this one night makes all that lost time worthwhile?"

Closing a hand lightly around her throat, he brought her mouth to his. "Because this one moment makes all that lost time worthwhile."

With a sound like a purr, Raven splayed her fingers over his stomach. "In that case, McInnis, you're gonna love what the next moment holds."

AIDAN DREAMED ABOUT a beautiful raven with eyes like green mist and legs that went on forever. Unfortunately, he also dreamed about more malevolent ravens carrying guns and knives and porn magazines.

A man's voice said, "Jason," over and over in his sleeping mind. Finally, thankfully, the only Raven he cared about returned to whisper gently in his ear.

"If you're going to talk in your sleep, I'd rather you said my name than Jason Demars's." Then she kissed his cheek and gave his butt a slap. "Wake up, Aidan. Someone's banging on the door."

He forced his eyes open to a rapier-sharp beam of light. "Jesus!" And slammed them shut. "Whoever it is, shoot him. And while you're at it, blow away the road crew that's jackhammering inside my head." The simple act of rolling onto his back required a gargantuan effort. "What the hell kind of wine was that?"

"It's called Raven's Blood." She gave him a kiss and a

sympathetic smile. "Exclusive to Raven's Cove and extremely potent. Still a fist banging on the door, Lieutenant. I can't get my suitcase unlocked, and I'm not opening to anyone wearing just your shirt."

This visit, he decided grimly, had better be worth a sledgehammer to the skull.

Dragging on jeans, he let his hair hang in his eyes to help ward off the light and, after groping his way through the RV, opened the door. "What?" he demanded without preface.

The man who'd given them the Mason jar of liquor at the campfire stood there, his knuckles raised. "Oh, hello. Sorry to wake you, but one of your neighbors said you were staying here."

Aidan braced his hands on the door frame and hoped he wouldn't go blind from the foggy daylight. "Do you want me or the reverend?"

"If you're a cop, I want you."

He swore his way through a nod. "I'm a cop. Is there a problem?"

"I'm not sure, not entirely. A couple of tenters were walking in the rain late last night, and they thought they saw something where the food people are set up."

Because the man's braid was dripping, Aidan stepped back and let him inside. "Company," he warned Raven, then gritted his teeth as a wave of nausea swamped him simply for raising his voice. "Go on," he told the man.

"They said it wasn't much of a thing, just a tent flap lifting and then the silhouette of the fish man jumping up, grabbing a rifle and shouting. They couldn't hear what he said."

"Is that it?"

"From the tenters' perspective, yeah. The light that had been on went out, so they kept walking. Here's the thing, though. I went to the market area about an hour ago to buy some oysters, and I couldn't find the fish man anywhere. His truck's there, and so are his coolers and grill, but he's gone. Now, I know he could be hiking in the woods, but why would he do that when he knew I was coming by at 8:00 a.m. to pick up a big order? He promised he'd have the oysters I wanted packed and ready to go. But they weren't. Also, his tent was only zipped partway closed, and a lot of his camping gear was wet."

Aidan rubbed his aching forehead. "What time is it now?"

"A little after nine. I spent an hour searching the woods, but I didn't find him."

"Have you talked to anyone except the people who saw him last night?"

"There aren't many others out and about. It's a soggy morning, and everyone knows we've got a big night ahead. I figure most folks aren't in a rush to get started early."

No argument there, Aidan thought. "Yeah, okay, I'll take a look."

When the man left, Aidan turned and drilled his fingers into his throbbing forehead. A few seconds later, Raven appeared at the bedroom door wearing narrow jeans, high black boots and a tight red T, with a V down to there.

Grimacing over pain that was unlikely to give him a break, Aidan asked, "Do you even know what the phrase 'fighting fair' means?"

"Yes, I do, and I practice it—with everyone except you, Steven and weaselly hit men who can't keep their hands to themselves." She moved toward the kitchenette. "Do you want coffee or wine? Hair of the dog," she added when he lasered her a lethal look.

"Coffee, extra strong, and get your jacket. I need your eyes."

"So I heard that man right, then. The fish guy's missing."

With an efficiency he'd always admired, she measured out dark-roast coffee and set the machine to brew. "Hair of the dog would probably work better, but as a physician, I'm disinclined to encourage unhealthy habits. Did I also hear him mention a rifle?"

Aidan closed his eyes. "You did."

"Lovely. Isn't it wonderful when a day starts like this?"

"Like what? With a hangover from hell or a potential disaster?"

"Either or." She placed a shot glass in his fingers and closed them around it. "But most of all with a doctor telling the man she loves to ignore everything she's ever said about what not to put in his body and, just this once, because she's very afraid he's going to need it, to drink up."

FIFTEEN MINUTES AND one damp hike later, Raven decided that Aidan was the coolest cop ever. To combat the morning chill, he wore a dark denim shirt, a black biker jacket, black boots, jeans and, despite the gloom, a pair of rockstar sunglasses over his still-bleary eyes.

"If it helps, I feel really guilty." She speed dialed Steven's cell phone. "I honestly forgot how strong that wine is."

He sized up the fish man's tent from the outside. "On the flip side, it explains the exaggerated wink I got from your cousin."

"Actually, the wink was a sexual reference. The elbow to your ribs was for the wine... Steven's not answering. I'll have to go to the cottage."

Aidan went down on one knee to inspect the tent flap. "Call Gaitor first."

"I did. He sounds groggier than you. I have a feeling the fishermen showed up at Blume House with some Raven's Blood of their own."

"Yeah, well just so you know, hair of the raven is at best half a cure."

Raven kissed the top of Aidan's head while she dialed Rooney's number. "Did I mention, sorry?" She waited, then sighed in frustration.

"Grandpa's phone's off." While Aidan did his cop thing, she pivoted on her heel. "You know, I get the weirdest feeling when I'm in this part of the clearing."

Aidan glanced at her. "Weird as in the evil spirit's lurking in the shadows, or something else?"

"Something else. It happened yesterday when I was with you, and briefly again when Steven and I were returning to the campsite from the crypt. Now, third time here, same feeling."

"Can you describe it?"

She thought for a moment. "It's not like I'm being watched. I recognize that one. It's more about a displaced sense of familiarity."

"With the clearing or some related aspect?"

"I don't know, that's what's weird about it. If it's déjà vu, no big worry. If it's one of those freaky ancestral traits my mother insists every Blume with Hezekiah's blood possesses, I want an exorcist."

She heard the faint amusement in Aidan's voice. "Seeing as the weird thing only happens when you're in this area, I'd go with déjà vu and worry more about what you can't feel."

"That remark," she decided, "comes very close to sounding like a portent of doom." When he went into the tent ahead of her and immediately swore, she summoned a benign smile. "And as the portent slowly fades, a living, breathing nightmare is born. Please tell me the man's not lying dead under his sleeping bag."

"He's not here, Raven." Aidan went to his haunches. "But his rifles are."

Fear slithered through her stomach. "Rifles—as in more than one?"

"Three that I can see. Two DMRs—designated marksman—and an M4 assault rifle."

"That does not sound good." She noted that a battery lamp had also been knocked over and currently lay in a puddle of rainwater.

"His sleeping bag's gone." Aidan lifted the air mattress, let it fall. "No blankets in sight. There's a half-drunk mug of beer and five oyster shells on the camp stool." He stood. "Is anyone outside?"

She glanced backward through the opening. "The Mason jar man's heading this way. One of the other food stalls is up and running, and the raven dog lady's lowering the side of her truck." She sighed. "We really need proper names for these people."

Five minutes later, thanks to Guy, the Mason jar man, they were introduced to Joanne, the raven dog lady and Fred, the black cotton candy man.

"I called him a lot of uncomplimentary things," Joanne admitted when Aidan questioned her, "but his name, well, he told you, it's Herron. Phil Herron, I think."

"When did you last see him?" Aidan asked.

"I'm not sure. Maybe ten o'clock last night. We took our time closing down because we figured on a late start today. There wasn't much business once the rain started, but you know how it is, we jabbed at each other, so the time passed quickly enough." The lines bracketing her mouth deepened and she turned, patting her chest as she thought back. "I did come out for a late cigarette—not sure what time, after midnight—and for a moment, I thought there was a man in front of Herron's tent. Then, poof, he was gone."

Raven frowned. "Gone inside, or gone away?"

"Not there anymore—if he ever was. The rain was pouring down and to be honest, I wasn't terribly interested. Still..." She huffed out an impatient breath. "Okay, here's the thing. If you asked me to describe the guy, I'd say he was wearing a long, dark coat and a big hat." She held up a hand. "Again, I didn't much care, but I remember thinking, he reminded me of that crazy preacher we talked about yesterday, the one they call Reverend Alley."

Chapter Thirteen

"No." Adamant, Raven yanked the bandage from her cousin's shoulder. "I don't care what that woman says, Gaitor is not working for Johnny Demars."

"Ouch." Steven glared at her. "Did I say he was?"

"You asked me if he could be. It's the same thing." She bent to inspect the bullet wound. "There's no sign of infection. You'll be doing push-ups in a few days."

"I'd believe that if the expression on your face didn't suggest you're tempted to put a bullet in my other shoulder. I'm not even the dreaded messenger here, Raven. Why are you so pissed about a vague allegation?"

Why was she? Raven wondered. She hunted for a fresh roll of gauze. "Because of George, I guess. And partly because you told me Fergus is off somewhere with Grandpa. And even though I don't believe Gaitor's a bad guy, I've got this microscopic seed of doubt in my mind now, and it extends to Fergus by association."

"Do you know where Gaitor is at the moment?"

"Last time I spoke to him, he was at Blume House and not quite awake. But when Aidan and I went up there after we talked to Joanne—she's the food vendor with the silver truck—he was gone. One of the men who spent the night at Blume House said somebody called right after I hung up. Gaitor left a few minutes later, but he didn't say who he talked to or where he was going."

"Huh."

She narrowed her eyes. "What does that mean?"

"Nothing, as long as you've got those stiletto scissors in your hand."

An artless smile tugged on her lips. "I don't stab irritating cousins with scissors, Steven." A twinkle appeared. "As a rule. I also don't suspect Gaitor of selling out, and I'm really not worried about Fergus being with Rooney, but it's another question added to a list of questions that keeps growing rather than shrinking."

"I'll accept that answer." But she noticed he kept a wary eye on the scissors. "Where's Aidan?"

"In the front yard, trying to track Gaitor down by phone."

"I thought maybe he didn't like blood."

"Only blood of the Raven's Cove vineyard variety."

"Ah, well, in that case, he might want to avoid the Reenactment tonight."

"Where's it taking place?"

"It traditionally unfolds at the town theater. However, since the theater has limited space, the mayor and council opted to play it out up on the ridge this year. They've got fireworks planned and a band—heavy on the bass drums for drama—coming in from the county seat. The whole thing's too loosely organized for my liking, but as events go, ours is still in the grass roots stage. One thing's sure, this Reenactment will be the most elaborate to date."

"Sounds intriguing. What if it rains?"

He shrugged. "Bring an umbrella. I made it crystal clear to everyone involved that Blume House is off-limits for any and all Ravenspell events. Of course that was before Aidan came back to life, and I got shot so a crime lord could make some puffed-up point."

Guilt twisted like a knife in Raven's stomach. "I really am so sorry about all the horrible things that have happened to you. I'm the one Demars wants, and you're the one who keeps getting hurt."

He dismissed her with a wave. "Don't sweat it, cousin. Just beat the bastard at his own game, and I'll be happy. Now, before you wrap me up again like a half-done mummy, talk to me about this missing fish man. Are you sure the woman who claims to have seen Gaitor as Reverend Alley at his tent can be trusted?"

"She didn't ask for trust, Steven. As for the fish man, all I can tell you is that his name's Phil Herron, and there's a strong possibility that he's the second of Demars's hit men."

"Hope so." Her cousin craned his neck and made a disgruntled sound. "Oh, great, Aidan's heading this way, looking very coplike and intense."

Raven tied off and snipped the gauze. When Aidan came in, she assessed his mood-darkened features. "Does that thundercloud expression mean you didn't locate Gaitor?"

"No, he's with a group of Ravenspell die-hards. They're trying to define the outer limits of the evil spirit's territory."

"Odd way to start a day. Why the face?"

He came around behind her. "I used your iPhone to place the call."

"Which is scowl-worthy because?"

"Right after it ended, a message appeared for you."

An icy finger trailed along her spine. But she maintained her composure and took the device. The message was simple, straightforward and terrifying.

Evil is as Evil does,
Raven Blume.
My son is dead, so you are dead.
An eye for an eye.

THE FOG GREW THROUGHOUT the morning. The chill within
it seeped into Raven's bones, and nothing Aidan or Steven said could chase it away.

Feeling moody now herself, she opted for a walk on
the beach over lunch in town.

There was something strangely soothing in the soft
shades of gray that enveloped her. Sky, cliffs, sand and
water bled together beneath swirling layers of mist. A
ghostly backdrop, she reflected, for the macabre reenactment of Hezekiah Blume's legendary transformation.

"You've gone quiet," Aidan remarked when they
reached the water's edge. "You know I won't let Demars
hurt you."

She gave a small laugh, gazed out to sea. "I'm not
worried about me. You know that—or you should. It's
the tone of Demars's text message that's so unsettling. It
feels like he's saying, *Here we are, Raven, you and me,
and we're getting this done today.* I know you, Aidan.
You'll die for real if you think it's the only way Demars
can be stopped. You'll kill him, he'll kill you and I'll go
on living." Barefoot, with her jeans rolled up and a boot
in each hand, she walked through the wet sand and lap-
ping ocean water. "Does that really sound fair to you?"

"As your husband and the man who loves you, I'd have
to say, yeah, it pretty much does. I'm the one who shot
Jason, Raven. Why should you pay the price for that?"

"Because I love you right back. And you were trying
to shoot him in the arm. It's not your fault he jumped
sideways at the last second."

"I should have aimed lower, gone for his leg."

"Leaving his shooting arm free to kill one of the cashiers." She stopped walking and faced him in the fog. "I don't want you to die for me. I don't want anyone to die for me."

Aidan stared into her eyes. "It bothers you, doesn't it? Gaitor," he clarified, and smiled when she hissed out a breath. "I'm not so hungover I can't follow your train of thought. Joanne thinks she saw him outside a missing man's tent, and now you're wondering if maybe Gaitor knows where the missing man is."

"Hit man," Raven corrected.

"Alleged hit man. We've got three rifles. That's not proof of a crime or even the intent to commit one."

"Maybe Gaitor found proof. Not that I want him to have acted on it, but thinking he made a hit man disappear is preferable to considering the possibility that he could be on Demars's payroll."

"Were you considering that possibility?"

"Yes—no." She rocked her head. "Maybe. For about a tenth of a second when Steven suggested it. The other thing, though—the idea that he made some kind of discovery about Phil Herron and decided to handle it in his own Gaitor way—that one stuck around a bit longer. We both know he learned how to police in a different era than you. And I'm not completely convinced you wouldn't have done something to the guy yourself given half a chance. But in the end, I came to the conclusion that you'd both suck it up and follow proper procedure. So, having reaffirmed Gaitor's status as a good guy, why do you think he was outside Phil Herron's tent last night?"

"That could have been anyone. Herron's tent is fifty

yards from Joanne's truck. It was dark, it was raining, and the person she saw was wearing black."

"All stellar points." A little surprised by an object slowly coming into view, she squinted forward. "Is that an old dory?" Aidan's uncomprehending expression made her grin. "A dory's a flat-bottomed boat."

"And you couldn't have just used the word *boat?*"

"I could have, except it's a dory, and you should be Irish enough to know the difference. Whatever you call it, being half-buried in the sand, it looks more like a beached whale than a watercraft. I'm surprised some kid hasn't…"

She trailed off as they drew closer, and the weathered hull came into focus.

Objects washed ashore with the tide, Raven realized over the building roar of blood in her ears. And they didn't always wash out again.

Like the arm and head barely visible around the splintered bow. The bloated arm and head of the man who'd gone missing from his tent last night.

Phil Herron.

THE MAN WAS DEAD. Anyone with eyes could see that. Unfortunately, both of Herron's eyes were missing, as was the back of his skull.

Raven knelt in the sand, a yard and half from the corpse and said nothing. But Aidan knew what she was thinking.

Taking her by the arms, he turned her until she looked at him. "This is not your fault. You need to understand that."

"I'm not blaming myself, not really. But I am confused. I thought maybe he'd faked his own disappearance to throw us off. Now? No idea. You?"

"Nothing that works start to finish. If Herron worked for and was killed by Demars, he must have done, seen or heard something that threatened his boss."

"Maybe he saw Demars's face," Raven speculated. "Automatic response? Shoot out his eyes. It could be a symbolic statement—vicious, but appropriate from this particular murderer's point of view."

Aidan's own eyes hadn't stopped moving. He scanned what he could see—not much—of the ridge that towered over them. Too many places for a sniper to hide, he decided, and tightened his grip on her arms. "We need to get out of here."

Uncertain, she regarded the nearby rocks and boulders. "I thought the fog might hide us." She banged her forehead on his chest. "Why would I think that after everything that's happened?"

"Because you're a doctor, not a cop. Different mentalities." Even as he spoke, Aidan glimpsed a flash of metal in the spot where the cliff sank to its lowest point and the rocks speared upward like daggers. "Behind me, Raven." Shoving her down, he whipped out his gun.

The first shot struck the damaged end of the dory. The second ricocheted off the rock face behind it.

Wrapping her fingers around Aidan's ankle, Raven tugged him back. "Bullets won't penetrate the hull. If the shooter stays where he is, we'll be covered."

Outpowered, outpositioned and with only one additional ammo clip in his back pocket, Aidan went with her suggestion and hoped to hell the old wood was thick enough to hold back rifle fire.

More bullets zinged off the dory. Because swearing helped him think, he did so while he checked his gun.

Behind him, Raven patted his ankle and pulled the

backup from his boot. "Please tell me you can hit a distant target through the fog with a Glock."

"You can." He shoved the half-empty clip back in. "But you need luck to do it." He watched the swirling clouds of white. "Fog's getting patchy. He's using the breaks to scope us."

"Can we get to those rocks?"

"Maybe." Two bullets embedded in the hull, then two more. "But that's where he'll expect us to go."

Another shot blasted the tip off the jutting cliff wall.

"We have to do something, Aidan. He's not going to run out of ammunition—oh, yuck, dead hand." She shoved Herron's lifeless fingers away. "All we've got are the rocks."

"Seems like." Ridiculously unfocused, he gestured with his gun. "Did you really just get weirded out by a dead man's flesh?"

"Diagnostic physician," she reminded, "not a forensic pathologist. Dead flesh is gross and—wait a minute!" She hunted through her jacket pockets. "Where's my— Do you have my phone? Give it," she said when his brows came together. She ducked automatically as two more bullets flew past. "I'll call Steven. He knows Blume House almost as well as Rooney does. There might be a way to get inside from out here. Prohibition, pirates, fortunes to be made, huge property to maintain—it's possible. No Blume was ever a paragon of virtue."

Aidan had his hand on her iPhone when he heard the tone that signaled an incoming text message. Lifting his eyes briefly to the fog shrouding the cliff, he read the four chilling words that had appeared on the screen.

Tick, tock
Tick, tock

THERE WERE AS MANY as five ocean-side access points, Steven informed her, but the only one he could direct them to had caved in several years before.

"He's calling Rooney." Raven pulled on her boots while the words of the text message repeated in her head. "How long's it been since we heard a shot?"

"Two minutes."

"It feels more like two hours." Her cell rang, and she answered. "Steven?"

"No, it's Gaitor. You sound shaken, Raven. Is something wrong?"

Aidan took the phone. "Where are you?"

"On my way back to the campsite from town. What's going on?"

"Are you alone?"

"No, I'm with Fergus and Rooney."

"Rooney!" Raven grabbed Aidan's hand, yanked it toward her. "Gaitor, ask him how we can access Blume House from the beach. We're about six hundred yards north of Raven's Ridge. Tell him Aidan and I need to get into the house—now."

It took a minute, time Raven knew they didn't have, but finally, her great-grandfather came up with a landmark she could identify through the fog. She followed a jagged crevice up the wall to a misshapen rock formation.

"We called it the Cave of Lost Souls back in the day," Rooney revealed. "Place is full of sinkholes, skinny bridges and passageways that lead to nowhere, but if your eyes are sharp, you won't get lost because there's a raven's feather printed on the wall every ten feet or so. They'll lead you right up into the house."

"I hope it's a Braille feather," Raven said as she ended the call. "I didn't bring a flashlight."

"I did." She watched Aidan size up the run they'd need

to make and the timeworn ledges they'd need to climb to reach the mouth of the cave. "You go first. I'll cover you. The fog'll help."

"But…"

"When you reach the cave, you can use that protrusion on the side to cover my back on the off chance he decides to go for me."

Did she have a choice? His backup in hand, she gave him a kiss, took a deep breath and, when Aidan tapped her butt, ran for the cliff wall.

Demars's response was instantaneous, a rapid onslaught of rifle fire, that, unfortunately, came from a lower position than before. Aidan fired back, and between the two weapons, each blast overlapped and created deafening distorted echoes.

Raven couldn't stop the thoughts flying through her head. She saw red eyes, then no eyes, Weasel's thin face and Herron's bloated one. She saw Gaitor with a beard and Fergus tiptoeing through Blume House, Steven injured and George as a ghost. Superimposed over all of that, however, she saw Aidan, and she vowed, as she clawed her way up the rugged cliff, that he would not die for her a second time.

A bullet bounced off the wall near her shoulder. Another narrowly missed her head. Every time Demars fired, Aidan answered back—and she wasn't sure he was doing so from the beach.

Her palms scraped and her nerves raw, Raven finally hoisted herself onto the ledge outside the cave. She was on her knees with her gun out when someone touched her shoulder from behind.

"It's me." Aidan trapped the swinging gun barrel with one hand and the back of her head with the other. "You climb like a mountain goat, Raven." He kissed her hard and deep. "I almost couldn't keep up."

"I knew it." She shook away the spinning heat. "You didn't wait. And don't tell me you weren't at risk because I'm the one he's after."

"I don't have to tell you what you already know." He kissed her again. "We're not safe yet, angel. Let's go."

Another flurry of shots erupted.

"This really sucks," she began, then spied the blood on Aidan's wrist and grabbed his hand.

"It's nothing," he promised. "A bullet nicked me on the way up. Trust me, the man had his sights on your back."

What could she do, Raven thought, but grit her teeth and let him propel her through the narrow opening?

Tendrils of fog trailed them into a dark, wet void where drips of water echoed as loudly as their footsteps. The halogen beam from Aidan's flashlight illuminated the blackness ahead. Recalling Rooney's words, she searched the walls and located a single black feather outlined in red. A moment later, she heard a scrape on the rocks behind them and froze.

"It's only bats. Keep going." Aidan's calm tone helped her beat the fear back.

She found another feather, then a third and a fourth. She also heard more scrapes on the cavern walls.

Her heart pounded. Demars was in here with them, he must be. But they'd turned two corners already and climbed at least twenty feet, so he might not know exactly where they were.

The feathers led them on a twisty upward path. The shadows became grotesque monsters. Once, Raven set her hand on a sleeping bat and was barely able to swallow the scream that leaped into her throat.

"Do you hear someone breathing?" she whispered at length.

"No, but if your mind needs to visualize something, go with Hezekiah in protective raven state."

"That does not make me feel better, Aidan. Hezekiah's about as far from a guardian angel as any legendary creation can g-get." The last word emerged on a stuttering gasp as she went to take a step and encountered nothing but air. Aidan snagged her waist, but not before her heart shot into her throat and her stomach dropped straight to her toes.

Eyes closed, she struggled to control her breathing. "How—far—down?" she managed to ask.

"Too far" was all Aidan said, but she heard anger now under the calm.

Raven took a moment to will her pulse rate down, blocked the echoing scrapes of God knows what behind them and squeezed the arm still wrapped like a steel band around her waist. "We've come a long way up and gone hundreds of yards south. We should be close to the subcellar by now."

He loosened his grip, kept his light angled down. "Why a subcellar, I'm pretty sure I don't want to know?"

She tossed him a deliberately teasing grin. "The usual reasons. Pirate stuff, illegal shipments of rum and brandy, maybe a few other commodities from the Caribbean."

"Jesus, Raven. Did anyone in your early American family operate within the confines of either church or state laws?"

"I think one of Hezekiah's cousins returned to Europe and became a monk, but that's about it…" She stopped moving, set her hand on yet another feather. "I distinctly heard a footstep—not sure from which direction."

He nodded, shone the flashlight beam ahead. "All we can do is keep going."

As reassuring as that wasn't, Raven knew they had no alternative. She continued along the feather trail. Two hundred feet farther on, they reached one of the dreaded skinny bridges.

"Don't worry, I've got you."

"Great. Who's got you?" She looked into the blackness behind them. "Was that a footstep or a scrape? I can't tell where the sounds are coming from anymore, let alone what they might actually be."

"Probably a good thing at this point." He ran his light along a narrow strip of rock. "Bridge is a twenty-foot span of rock. Not too bad."

Not bad if a person had suction cups on her feet, Raven thought. Boots with heels didn't inspire quite as much confidence.

Focusing, she set her sights solely on the path of Aidan's beam and didn't breathe until they reached the other side.

Leaning into his chest, she murmured, "My hair'll be snow-white by the time we get out of here. Where's the wall gone?"

He played the light to his left. "This way."

If he said more, Raven didn't hear it. A sharp corner appeared in front of them. She spied a shadow and a blur of black as someone turned that corner and crashed into her.

As startling as the collision was, her attempt to avoid the hands that immediately reached for her sent her staggering sideways. Not into Aidan, her shocked mind realized, but straight into the chasm they'd just crossed.

Chapter Fourteen

"I'm sorry, Raven." Gaitor's face under his beard was ashen. "I came down to meet you, to help you if I could, and instead I almost killed you." He mopped his neck and blew out a dry breath. "Your reflexes are quick as ever, partner. I thought she was a goner."

Raven rubbed her wrist where Aidan's strong fingers had caught her and pulled her until she was out of the yawning black pit and safely back on solid rock.

"Please tell me you're not hurt." Although it had taken them fifteen minutes to access the subcellar after her fall, Gaitor's tone told Raven he was still badly shaken.

Feeling steadier out of the cave, she patted his knee. "I'm honestly not hurt." A sense of mischief crept in and she smiled. "I might have a dislocated shoulder if I hadn't lost those two pounds."

As she'd hoped, Aidan's lips twitched. "Pretty sure you've lost two more by now."

"If dodging bullets didn't send the stress meter off the scale, I might be onto something.... What?" She frowned when he got to his feet. "Are we leaving already?"

"Scraping sounds—someone else's in the cave," he reminded.

Gaitor buttoned his coat. "I was moving semi-quickly

through the tunnel. Distortion, refraction—those sounds could have been me."

"They could also have been rodents." Aidan led the way up a rickety ladder staircase. "Or Johnny Demars."

"On the bright side," Raven said, and tested a sagging tread, "as real villains go, we're down to only him." When Aidan didn't respond, she hit his leg. "What does that mean?"

"Did I say something?"

"No, and that's the giveaway."

"Sorry, angel, I'm not as convinced as you are that Demars is the only person we still need to worry about."

"Ask a stupid question." She blew out a breath. "Why?"

"Gut feeling."

Gaitor snorted. "I hate those damn things. Nine times out of ten, my instincts turn out to be nothing more than a greasy burger I shouldn't have eaten the night before. How many people could Demars reasonably bring with him, Aidan? Both his go-to assassins gone, and George got nailed right off the bat."

Aidan shouldered the door open and stepped ahead of Raven into the marginally less musty main cellar. "Technically, Demars doesn't bring anyone, but to be on the safe side, he could have sent any number of snipers. From what we know about him, he could also walk up to any of those snipers, ask for directions, and they wouldn't have a clue who was doing the asking." When Gaitor grunted and jammed on his reverend's hat, he let his lips quirk. "Just saying."

Back in full disguise, the older man placed his hands on Raven's shoulders. "And he calls me gloomy. Rooney wants to talk to you. Something about a costume he'd like you to wear for the Reenactment."

She offered Aidan a bland smile. "Should I bother

having that chat, or will we be hiding out in the attic tonight?"

"We'll be hiding," Aidan agreed, "but not in the attic."

Gaitor dusted off his coat. "Let me know what you decide. Meanwhile, before the festivities commence, I have a bone to pick with a certain female hot dog vendor who needs glasses badly if she thinks she saw me anywhere near the clearing last night."

"She didn't come right out and accuse you of being there," Raven told him. "As Aidan said, it was dark and the person outside Herron's tent was wearing black. She could have seen anyone."

"Except she intimated it was me." Gaitor's lips flattened to a thin line. "I want to know why, and I want it straight from the horse's mouth. You need me in the meantime, Aidan, you've got my number." His parting smile was a mere show of teeth above his beard.

A curious chill rippled through Raven's bloodstream as Gaitor left. "Well, that's totally weird." She turned a full baffled circle. "I've got that freaky feeling again, and we're nowhere near the market stalls."

"Yeah? Huh. Can't imagine where a freaky feeling might stem from. Corpse on the beach, flying bullets, two near fatal missteps—nothing weird in any of that."

"True. We're also in Raven's Cove, and it's Ravenspell."

"Whatever that means."

"There are real facts and Cove facts, Aidan, and I'm a Blume. Now, getting back to the beach and the little matter of Herron's body. We can't leave it there for kids playing pirate to find."

"Even though we're in Raven's Cove?"

"You need to call the county sheriff. It's not right to keep hiding dead bodies and tell ourselves we'll deal with them later."

"You've obviously never dealt with a county sheriff before. It can be a smooth road, or one so full of potholes you wish you'd never turned onto it."

Chuckling, she patted his cheek. "You're an excellent driver, Lieutenant. If anyone can navigate potholes, it's you. I only wish getting around Rooney would be as easy."

"What's to get around, other than the costume?"

"I'm not well versed on the specifics of the Reenactment, but I know it involves a lot of people dressed as ravens, one particular person decked out as Hezekiah in human and bird forms, a good spirit, the silhouette and snakelike voice of the evil that infected him, and of course, the townspeople he murdered at the beginning of the tale."

"So far, so theatrical. What's the catch?"

Her lips tipped up. "There aren't enough actors in Raven's Cove to fill the roles. Means they have to use locals. Rooney's in charge of recruiting modern-day versions of the murder victims."

Aidan's eyes narrowed on her deliberately neutral features. "And that involves you how?"

Determined to lighten the mood, she strolled up to him, touched her tongue to her upper lip and slid a provocative finger along his throat to his collarbone.

"Story goes that the last person Hezekiah killed before he repented was a man named Zachary Blume. Zachary was Hezekiah's cousin." She kissed the pulse point at the base of his throat. "As coincidence would have it, he was also the newly arrived town doctor."

It would be done tonight, Demars vowed, while people were distracted and costumed role players ruled the ridge beyond Blume House.

No way to control the peripherals, of course, but improvisation had worked in the past.

Then there was the ace, cleverly tucked up and waiting to strike.

Visualizing the moment of Raven Blume's death, the crime boss whispered a scathing, "You'll know soon enough, Aidan McInnis, how it feels to lose the person you love above all else in life."

The cruel smile that formed felt as good now as it had twelve years ago.

Until Jason had discovered the truth.

A SHOWER, EVEN IN THE snug confines of Gaitor's RV, felt like heaven to Raven's abused muscles. Every part of her was either bruised, cut or scraped. She set the nozzle on Pulse, closed her eyes and zoned out for ten exquisite minutes. Then she turned off the spray and was zapped straight back to cold, hard reality.

Voices trickled through the bathroom door. Aidan's, Gaitor's and occasionally Steven's. In snatches, she discovered that Aidan had in fact contacted the county sheriff about the dead people. He and Gaitor had removed Phil Herron's body from the beach and put it with Weasel's in the family crypt.

Aidan had also searched for and found a spent cartridge in the sand near the rock wall. He and Gaitor agreed it had been fired from an M16 assault rifle, which they believed was the weapon that had blasted twin holes through Phil Herron's eye sockets.

Shuddering that grisly visual away, Raven slicked on a layer of orchid-scented lotion.

Tick, tock. Tick, tock...

Although she struggled to shut them out, the words of Demars's text message resounded in her head. They were nearing thunderous proportions, when the bathroom door opened.

Snapping her head up, Raven shook the damp hair from her eyes. And breathed out when she saw Aidan. "You know, I'm so used to my heart wanting to bash through my rib cage, it's starting to feel like a normal state. Uh…" She flicked a questioning finger at the living room.

Aidan's dark eyes sparkled. "Gone."

Dropping her hand, she smiled. "Like you'd come in here if they weren't. Sorry. My brain's running ten steps behind my mouth at the moment."

"Yeah?" The sparkle deepened and stirred her amusement.

"You do know it's getting late," she warned when he pushed off from the frame. "We don't have time to be— well, God."

He swallowed her laughing protest, taking her mouth and booting the door closed with his foot. "There's always time to get wet and naked, angel."

"Oh, well, you're running way behind me there." Easing back, she began unsnapping the buttons of his shirt. "Guess it's your turn to do the catching up."

"Trust me, Raven, I'm very up. And I've been caught for years."

"In that case…" She tore the rest of the buttons open, hooked a bare leg around his hips and dived in. "Let's get Ravenspell started with a steamy Reenactment of our own."

AFTER TWO YEARS OF NO SEX, then eighteen hours of little else, Raven's mind was buzzed and her body gloriously numb.

They ate a lunch-dinner combo cold from the fridge,

but avoided the half bottle of Raven's Blood still sitting next to the fireplace. Her great-grandfather called to tell her there were costumes waiting up at Blume House. Because the absentee deputy had been slotted to play Hezekiah, he wanted Aidan to pinch-hit, with Raven cast in the surprising role of the good spirit. Better in the story than on the sidelines, was Rooney's sage philosophy.

The trick was to make it Aidan's, as well.

"Being a spirit, I could hang out in the background and leave the spotlight stuff to the more seasoned players. As Hezekiah, you could make sure—" She positioned and repositioned her hands. "Hmm, well, maybe not."

"Definitely not." Dressed in fresh jeans and an even cooler jacket than before, Aidan stuffed the Glock in his waistband and strapped on his backup. "We don't know what Demars's overall plan might entail. The best we can do is control as much as possible on our end."

"Which is why you're okay with me being part of the performance."

"Sort of okay with it," he corrected. "The last thing I intend to do is let myself be distracted by spotlights and actors and someone telling me to look tormented."

"You know, I get that, I really do." She grinned at him via the bedroom mirror. "It's just that you're so perfect for the part."

"You see me as a homicidal maniac, looking to the dark side for personal power?"

"Anguished homicidal maniac. Hezekiah had emotional and mental issues."

"Bull." He sent her a slow smile. "That's you, his descendants, prettying the story up. He went looking to be possessed because he was pissed off about some aspect of his life, and he got his wish."

"You'd have made one truly lousy psychiatrist, McInnis."

"Glad to hear it." Sliding a hand over her hair, he tipped her face up to his for a kiss. "Tell Rooney I'll play one of the background ravens and make sure he gives Fergus and at least three other large men the same outfits. Now, talk to me about the good spirit's costume."

"It's a silver cloak." She shot him a suspicious look through her lashes. "Why are you being so amenable?"

"Full head mask?"

"Yes."

"Hood?"

She crossed her arms. "Yes, there's a hood but, no, I'm not calling Rooney until you tell me what's going on in that cop brain of yours. I know you're thinking I'd make an easy target in a billowy silver cape, so what's the deal? Will I be wearing a bulletproof bodysuit underneath?"

"If we can get our hands on one, absolutely. If not, we'll settle for mixing things up a bit."

A light winked on. "Ah, got it. Mixing—as in I won't really be playing the good spirit." Moving her lips into a blithe smile, she replied along with him, "No, you won't. Steven will."

Aidan chuckled. "Exactly how do you do that?"

"I'd say I was psychic, except in this case, I heard Steven while I was drying off in the bathroom. He said he wants it made clear before he goes front and center onstage that there's been a last-minute substitution. I didn't know what he meant at first, but being around you, I've learned to play catch-up. Aidan, what if Demars shoots the good spirit anyway, just for the hell of it."

"Italian mother, angel. It wouldn't be ethical."

"And if he lapses in that area?"

"The sheriff's office is trying to locate a bulletproof

vest." He trapped her chin for another kiss. "Steven's fine with the idea, and I don't intend to give Demars any clear shots. The plan is to close on him while he's setting up. There are a limited number of vantage points for a shooter on the ridge."

"Meaning the ball's in our court?"

"Meaning if we don't do something here and now, he'll have the element of surprise entirely back on his side."

Working through her frustration, Raven picked up the mini cassette recorder. "This has to be something, don't you think, because a person like Weasel wouldn't own or use such an outdated device. And why would he carry it around with him even if he did have a bent for old technology?" She played the tape again, heard the man at the end offer a weary "Jason…" But still no face materialized.

"It'll drive you crazy if you let it." Aidan zipped his jacket. "It's like a yo-yo in your brain. Yes, I recognize him, no, I don't."

"Diagnosing unusual problems is my area of expertise," Raven pointed out. "I'll listen to it again while we drive to town."

"We're driving to town?"

"I'm told the pharmacist wants to see me." Humor nudged in. "Medicine is kind of why I came to Raven's Cove, Aidan. It shouldn't take long, and, who knows, maybe the bumpy ride will shake loose a useful memory."

"Be nice."

Halting on the threshold, she looked back. "Do you think he'll come after me during the Reenactment?"

"The play's an opportunity, and it strikes me that Demars is growing impatient. Whatever he does or doesn't do, I want to be prepared." He kissed her again, and something in his touch stilled the panic that wanted to rise. "One thing, I'm sure of is that I'm not going to let you or any member of your family die at the hands of Johnny Demars. No matter what the cost."

THE FACT THAT SHE believed him unsettled her sufficiently that she neglected to press for details. And not knowing was a situation Raven despised. She'd forfeited two years of her life because she hadn't known what Aidan and his captain had strategized. Unfortunately, by the time she firmed up her resolve, it was too late for explanations.

After a rushed trip to town, Gaitor and Steven met them in the clearing. Together, they joined the crowd swarming the repositioned market stalls.

Fred, the cotton candy man, had hauled Phil Herron's grill to the ridge and fired it up. Joanne was serving raven dogs and burgers by the score. Raven was about to order a bottle of juice when she spotted Guy, the hippie with the beard and braid, heading toward her. He shouted something she couldn't hear, then cut across the flat rock carrying a box of fruit-filled Mason jars.

"I'm giving miniature jars of my home brew to all the participants," he said with a grin that didn't quite stamp out the concern on his features. "Like any show, the Re-enactment must go on, even with Herron still MIA."

Raven summoned a casual "Oh, I'm sure he's around somewhere." She held up and studied the jar. "Is this the same thing I drank at the campfire?"

"You bet. Your friend Sylvie helped me put a batch of them together this afternoon. We went through multiple bottles of vodka. No half measures where I come from. You wanna strip the skin from a person's gullet, you get it done with the first swallow." Balancing his load, he raised a parting hand. "I'll collect the jar later. Enjoy."

She felt a movement near her shoulder while she unscrewed the lid.

"As a man of the cloth, Raven, I'm compelled to point out that drinking any substance guaranteed to disintegrate your vocal cords is not, under the circumstances, the wisest choice. Better hand it over."

"Says the man whose eyes in good light still resemble roadmaps." She swirled the fruity concoction. "Come on, Gaitor, this stuff has a decent first kick, but it's O'Doul's compared to Raven's Blood."

"News flash, your family wine has recently been added to our nation's top ten list of toxic substances."

"In that case, we're wasting time with bullets and strategy. All we really need to do is give Johnny Demars a bottle of Blood and scrape his remains off the ridge in the morning."

"You're joking, but it's a workable thought." He motioned at the silver truck. "I talked to my accuser. In her own I-hate-nut-ball-preachers way, she half apologized for any allegation she might have made. But she still believes she saw someone outside Herron's tent."

"Maybe it was Fred wearing a cloak made of black cotton candy." Raven regarded the woodland trees. "It's getting dark—well, darker. The die-hards have their blankets and chairs spread around the so-called stage. Another thirty minutes, and the ravens will begin to circulate."

"Is this what you call an interactive event?"

"Interactive and largely impromptu. According to Grandpa, there's not much of a script. Everyone here is familiar with 'The Raven's Tale.' Equally familiar with 'The Soldier's Tale'—probably not so much."

"The faithful know it."

She dropped the miniature Mason jar into his gloved hand. "I guess that would make me an unfaithful Blume, despite my line of descent. I only hope the evil that was left behind doesn't decide to aid Johnny Demars in his quest." Her eyes skimmed the growing crowd. "Have you spotted anyone suspicious?"

"Not a soul, and I've been watching closely. Careful, folks," he cautioned as an enthusiastic group of campers jostled past.

At the tail end of the rush, an arm descended on her shoulders. "Costume's waiting up at Blume House, Raven," Aidan said in her ear. "You put it on, sans mask and hood, head backstage—that would be in the trees— where you and your cousin will do a quick switch. We'll see what transpires from there."

More campers bumped her as they brushed by. "You won't let Demars hurt Steven, right?"

"The sheriff supplied us with a vest and two deputies. One of them will stick close to him. Five tough men, handpicked by your great-grandfather, will also be wandering around dressed as ravens. So will Fergus and I. Once you and Steven switch costumes, you're with me. I've shown you the sniper vantage points and three other potential sites. Fog's down to a light mist—not the best scenario, but not much we can do about it—and we're less than forty-five minutes from full darkness. Generators are up and running, spotlights are positioned around the perimeter. Our view of the high points should be good. Any last-minute questions?"

Shivering, she slipped her hands into the pockets of her jacket. "What if Demars manages to insinuate himself into the Reenactment?"

Aidan glanced at Gaitor as more people streamed past heading for the food. "We thought of that. It's why I want you with me. Are you ready?"

"Do ravens' feathers foreshadow death? Answer's yes," she stage whispered to a puzzled Gaitor.

His frown deepened. "I know about the feathers and

what awaits the recipient of them, Raven. I'm only surprised you'd use such a maudlin analogy."

"It is maudlin," she agreed. "But as analogies go, it's also completely appropriate."

Keeping her right hand steady, she removed it from her jacket pocket—and showed them the three black feathers someone in the crowd had slipped to her.

HE SLUNK ACROSS THE RIDGE with one and only one thought in his head—to find that perfect spot, set up and wait.

In a way—a rather large way, in fact—it was a shame Raven Blume had to die in order to settle a score, but like so many things in life, what had to be done had to be done. And in this case, there'd be an enormous personal reward at the end of it.

As darkness descended and the spotlights began to glow, he settled in his perch near the rock ledge that towered some twenty-five feet above the elevated stage.

He'd checked it out earlier and concluded it would work. Ravens nested in the trees that brushed this portion of the cliff, so there'd be irony as well as intelligence in the selection.

Everything about Raven's Cove centered around those big black birds. For most people, Hezekiah was the raven of interest. But for the man who detached himself from the excited crowd, the only Raven that mattered would be dead before her ancestor's legendary transformation.

He thought with mounting anticipation, *Let the game begin.*

Chapter Fifteen

The best-laid plans...

For some irritating reason, those words began whispering in Aidan's head the moment he and Raven separated. He could see her, and the myriad costumed ravens around her, but it didn't feel like enough. Not nearly enough right now.

The combined smells of cod and grilled burgers wafted past him, carried on the evening mist. He watched the back of Raven's cape as she made her way toward the stage where Fergus and two other men stood guard, and hoped the two-way radios they'd borrowed from the county sheriff's office weren't as crappy as they looked.

"Soon as Fergus heads for the trees, we'll know she's made the costume switch with Steven." Stationed several feet away, Gaitor pretended to read from his book on local lore. "Any movement in the high areas?"

"Not so far."

Gaitor turned a page, regarded the throng ahead of them. "Is there an official start to this thing, or does some random person just yell, 'Game on,' and the actors take it from there?"

"It's starting now." Aidan's eyes remained on the trees where one by one the main players emerged.

Without fanfare, a dozen ravens burst from the branches and vanished into the mist at full raucous caw.

"There's the good spirit." Gaitor sounded as relieved as Aidan felt. "And there goes Fergus to fetch Raven back."

The costumed birds traveled in pairs. Still, Aidan reflected, the best-laid plans…

He swore long and low.

Gaitor's head shot up. "What? Is there a problem?"

Amusement glimmered despite the circumstances. "Would I be standing here if there was? Lose the nerves, Gaitor, or we'll all be screwed."

"Worry about yourself, McInnis and leave…" He broke off when Aidan swore again. "Crissakes, what now?"

"High shadows are shifting at three o'clock. Circle toward them. I'll intercept Fergus."

He kept an unwavering eye on the big man and his smaller raven companion. "Meet me by Herron's grill," he said into his two-way, and watched Fergus immediately change direction.

So far, so good, Aidan told himself. But the best-laid… "Dammit, piss off," he snapped. He added, less testy, "Sorry, Fergus not you. Bring her to the grill."

The minute Fergus complied, Aidan drew Raven into a deep shadow and clasped her shoulders. "I need you to stay here, okay? Right here. Promise me you won't move."

She used the two-way in her head mask for the first time. "I won't move. Just don't forget about Steven."

"He's covered…. Say again, Gaitor?"

"The shadow shift you spotted was someone setting up for a photo shoot."

"False alarm," Aidan relayed to Raven and Fergus. He bumped his gaze from point to point. Nothing else stirred.

"Lieutenant McInnis?" A sea-roughened voice crackled over the headset. "Old Joe—Two Toes—just told me there's a guy sitting like a big Hezekiah raven in a pine tree on the north point. He's carrying a rifle."

"Where's the north point?" Aidan asked Raven.

She pivoted, aimed a feathery finger.

"On my way," he told the man. "Gaitor?"

"Halfway there already."

"Don't move," Aidan repeated, and took off to the sound of a low growl in her throat.

He shed the restrictive cloak and mask as he ran, but made sure his two-way remained intact. Gaitor puffed out a location, but with the north point in sight Aidan had already identified the only tree from which Demars could view the entire area.

Drawing his Glock, he headed for the top via a crude set of ledges.

An ancient but sturdy evergreen stood to his left. If he climbed to the summit he'd be parallel with the upper branches.

"Stop before you get to the top," he instructed Gaitor. "We might be able to cut off his escape if he runs."

A winded grunt he took for a yes came back to him.

Aidan set his sights on the target. But the fear of something screwing up continued to haunt him as he reached the high plateau.

"He's still there," one of Rooney's men said from below. "But he might be catching on. He's getting twitchy... No, wait, hell, he's turning jackrabbit."

Stuffing his gun, Aidan jumped to an outstretched limb. "Can you see him?" he asked Gaitor.

"He was climbing toward you," his partner shouted back. "But I can't see him now for the branches."

"Come on, you bastard." Aidan drew and readied his weapon. "All I need's a glimpse."

What he got instead was a blinding glare of light

beamed directly into his eyes as the spotlights made their first creaky revolution. Below him, he heard a rustle that quickly turned into a thrash of leaves.

Before he could react, a rifle butt slammed across his shin and almost cost him his balance. A second blow got him in the thigh, dangerously close to his groin. Even so, he squeezed off two silenced shots—and took a measure of grim satisfaction from the indrawn yowl of pain that reached him.

He knew right away he hadn't hit anything important, because after more thrashing, his quarry launched from the tree and landed hands and knees on the plateau.

"He's made the rock," Aidan warned Gaitor. "Can you cut him off?"

"Do my best, partner."

Unfortunately, the man did in fact move like a jackrabbit. He bounded downward from ledge to ledge, glanced at Aidan, who'd jumped from the tree after him and, ditching his rifle, zigzagged to the level ridge.

He was fast and nimble, Aidan gave him that. But he also thought in two dimensions and veered instinctively toward the woods.

Instead of pursuing him, Aidan stuck to the higher rock. "He's heading for the road," he said to Gaitor.

"Why go—through—the woods?" Gaitor puffed. "Why not just—never mind. You take the forest. I'll take the shorter route."

"Use Rooney's Jeep," Aidan told him. "Keys are inside."

"Good, thanks—I will. If you're right—we can squeeze him."

"Sounds like a plan."

Running on relatively flat ground was easy for Aidan, so much so that it allowed his brain to kick back into gear. Too bad every thought that formed did so in blinding red neon.

Too obvious…too predictable…not clever enough…

But then again, wasn't that why crime lords hired the Weasels and "big guys" of the world to do their killing? Because the pros knew how to avoid capture, while those who employed them might not be so savvy?

The runner darted through gullies and hopped over fallen logs, but Aidan suspected he was tiring. Even jackrabbits had their limits.

Unfortunately, so did cops who'd been dead for two years. A mile in, he opted to go with the odds. He waited for the man to pull up as they approached a wide stand of bushes, then, stopping, fired three shots into the mist.

The runner stiffened and spun in place. Several drunken steps later, he vanished into the darkness.

Aidan headed toward the greenery with caution. Tendrils of white twined about his ankles, but all he could hear were his own footsteps and half the insect population of Maine waking up for the night.

He expected the shots when he glimpsed the man down on one knee, his shoulder butted up against a rock smeared dark with blood.

Ducking behind a bush, Aidan called to him, "You can toss the gun or bleed out. Your choice."

"Go ahead and shoot, McInnis—if you've got the balls. I see your face or any other part of you, you're a dead man."

"You think?" Clearing the outer leaves, Aidan took aim, cursed the night mist and squeezed the trigger.

The man's body jerked. He'd worked himself to his feet, but Aidan's bullet threw him against the trunk of a poplar and sent his gun flying into the night.

"You know you have to kill me, right? I'll keep fighting you until you do."

"Why?"

"Because you murdered my kid, why the hell do you think?"

"You know what happened that night. Jason's dying wasn't part of any plan."

"He's dead all the same, isn't he?"

The sudden surge of motion came as no surprise. It irritated the hell out of him, but Aidan had already figured the guy was playing possum to some degree. He'd wanted a clear shot of his own. Hadn't gotten one, but like any shooter worth his salt, he'd taken a chance.

"Where are you?" Gaitor shouted the question through increasing static.

"No idea."

Back on the move, the man leaped left, somersaulted over a felled tree and barreled on.

"Take the next road that goes west, partner."

"I sent a sheriff's deputy after you," Gaitor returned. "Hope he's fit enough to keep up."

Aidan hoped he was fit enough to keep his quarry in sight, because there was no chance the guy would be exiting the woods anytime soon.

Another mile on, the runner veered right, halted abruptly and slipped out of sight behind a fat spruce. "Stop there, McInnis."

At least he was panting, Aidan thought as he bent at the waist to suck in badly needed air.

"Come one step closer—" the man emerged from the trunk as a silhouette "—and I'll drill the bitch."

Aidan's insides turned to liquid. Until his eyes cleared and he realized the woman who'd been yanked—bound, gagged and whimpering—into view had the wrong shape to be Raven. This woman's hair was short and her figure less curvy.

"Yes, you can see she's not your precious wife, but you wouldn't want this one's death on your conscience, either, would you?"

"Is this what you want?" Aidan called back. "To kill an innocent woman? A stranger?"

"Who I do or don't kill at this particular moment is entirely up to you, Lieutenant. You let me walk, I let her live. It's a fair exchange. Don't," he barked when Aidan's hand twitched. "You can't be stupid enough to think I don't have a gun stuck in her back."

"No, I'm not stupid enough to think that. Then again…"

When a twig snapped behind him, the man reacted instinctively, swinging his head around to find Gaitor standing several yards away.

Aidan knew he had him then, and fired off three rapid shots—one in the shoulder, one in the side, one in the leg.

A shocked snarl emerged as the man reared backward, released his hostage and dropped to the ground, jerking in pain.

His legs wobbling from exertion, Gaitor went to his knees to help the woman, hysterical now, while Aidan grabbed the fallen man by his jacket and flipped him onto his back.

"Hey, Guy." Crouching, he jammed his Glock under the beard of the braided hippie. "You're an agile bastard, I'll give you that."

"Hey yourself, Lieutenant." The man bit the words out on wheezing bursts of breath. "You move pretty well yourself."

When Gaitor pulled the gag from the woman's mouth,

Aidan realized that Guy's hostage was Sylvie, the blonde woman who'd helped him find Raven in the crypt.

Still on her butt, she caterpillar crawled away from her captor. "You should shoot him," she said with a quaver. "He's crazy, and I mean stark raving." She started to shiver. "I helped him bottle that fruit stuff he likes so much, and suddenly, out of nowhere, he shoves a knife under my chin and says his name's not really Biggs, it's Demars. Like it makes a difference what he calls himself when I figure he's gonna stick me."

Pounding footsteps approached and slowed. In the process of untying the ropes from Sylvie's ankles, Gaitor raised a hand. "It's okay, Deputy, we're good. McInnis and me got him."

The winded deputy bent for a look. "You might not have him for long if you don't get him to a hospital, sirs. Bangor should do since it seems like all three bullets passed right through."

The neon flashed a new and larger warning in Aidan's head. Something about this felt wrong. The reason slammed into him when he stood to stash his gun.

"Biggs," he repeated, and narrowed his eyes on Sylvie's face. "Is that what you said?"

"I said what he said. 'Call me Biggs,' he told me my first night here."

But that wasn't what he'd told Raven. "I'm Guy," he'd said outside Phil Herron's empty tent.

A tent that contained three rifles. The tent of a man who'd had his eyes shot out and his body dumped in the ocean.

"Biggs." Aidan spoke to Gaitor now. "Guy Biggs. He's George's 'big guy.' Jesus, Gaitor, he's not Johnny Demars. He's Demars's second hit man." Which meant, Aidan realized through a nightmarish haze of fear, that Demars was back on the ridge.

With Raven.

MOST OF THE PLAYERS wandered off the stage and into the audience at will. Only Hezekiah and the good and evil spirits had voices and were therefore required to stay put.

"The 'evil' actor sounds exactly like I figure a snake would sound." Fergus squirmed. "Low and hissy, like a trail of slime."

Raven rubbed her chilled arms. "My grandfather—my dad's father—sounded like that, and he wasn't even a Blume. Wonder what that says about his personality?"

Fergus followed her gaze. "You're worried, aren't you?"

"Very. Aidan would say I shouldn't be, but I can't help it. Johnny Demars is a shadow, Fergus. How do you capture a shadow?"

"You dip it in lead and make it so the shadow can't disappear." He shrugged a massive shoulder. "Gaitor told me that, once when I was a kid and I asked the same question. I thought it was kind of a cool idea. Er, do you think we can take our masks off now?"

"Probably." Not that she wanted to, but the last communication she'd heard on her crackling two-way had been a shout from one of the Reenactment ravens about a jackrabbit.

Fergus removed his feathered head. "That's better." He whooshed out a breath, inhaled deeply and coughed when his lungs filled with drifting grill smoke. "Aw, that's gross. I don't like fish, do you? I mean I know it's good for you, but it always tastes so—fishy."

Raven laughed at his expression. "You look like a baby

who's just swallowed a spoonful of mashed carrots and beets."

He brightened. "I could eat that before smoked salmon. My uncle loves smoked West Coast salmon."

"I know. I made sure it was served at Aidan's wake." She twirled her mask in agitation. "Where are they? And why did our stupid radios have to cut out?"

"Because they're old?"

His uncertain tone struck a humorous note. "Rooney's old, and he's still going strong. Why are you fidgeting?"

He squirmed again. "Ravenberry juice. It goes right through you."

"You mean you want to be excused."

"Only for a minute. I'll use the porta-john." He shuddered. "Just this once."

"You're a trouper, Fergus." Raven's grin was faint as her eyes rescanned the misty points of rock. "I'll wait for you here." Because—dumb, dumb, dumb—she'd promised Aidan she wouldn't move.

She hadn't, however, promised not to pace. Or to go over everything in her head for the umpteenth time.

George and Demars's two favorite hit men were dead. No, strike that. One hit man was dead. Phil Herron remained a question mark in Aidan's mind. No idea why.

Aidan believed that Demars had shot and killed Weasel. Weasel had had a mini cassette recorder and a tape in his backpack. A man's voice had said, "Jason..." at the end of a previously one way conversation.

Neither Raven nor Aidan recognized the voice. At least they couldn't connect it to anyone they'd met in Raven's Cove. That didn't mean Demars wasn't here, merely that they hadn't heard him speak. Or if they had, they didn't have enough of the taped voice to identify him.

Pressing her fingers to her temples, she walked back

and forth on the rocky ground and tried to unkink the thoughts jumbled together in her brain.

Outside view, inside view, abstract view, none of her usual clarification techniques worked. All she felt right now was terrified for Aidan's life and—weird, she realized suddenly. Now when had that sensation snuck back in?

Grill smoke blew by her in dense clouds. She couldn't imagine why that should intensify the feeling, but it did, so she went with it and concentrated.

In was like déjà vu, but not quite. Connected to the food stalls, but not really.

"Fish," she said softly. "Is it something to do with fish?"

A foggy, distant image floated just out of reach. Raven stood absolutely still, afraid if she moved, the partly formed memory would fade to black.

Was it a face, an object or both?

The grill smoke obscured her vision, yet in some strange way, it seemed to be aiding her memory.

Fergus's voice repeated, "Gaitor loves smoked salmon…"

Smoked salmon, smoke in the air. Smoke and trees blurring her mind, taking her to another place and time.

"You need to eat, dear…"

"You should dance, Raven…"

"Would you like a canapé, ma'am? The topping's smoked salmon…"

Like a light blinking on, the image solidified. It had a face, with features she recognized from two different places—Aidan's wake, and here.

She hitched in a shocked breath.

Wait though. Was this a valid memory or merely her overworked mind drawing false pictures?

Raven sensed a presence behind her a split second before a small, hard object dug into her spine.

"Hello, Raven," said a cold but familiar voice.

Valid, she realized as her lungs constricted and the blood in her veins turned to ice. Extremely valid.

The object—a gun not a knife—pushed in deeper. "Did you figure it out?" the voice asked. "Because you're not moving, not saying hello back and you don't seem the least bit surprised. I wondered if you might recognize me, but I told myself, no, she won't even remember the big parts of that day, let alone a single insignificant person inside one of the smaller ones. But I was wrong, wasn't I? You do remember some of those smaller pieces, and you've put the pertinent ones together with the here and now."

Raven wasn't sure how she found her voice, but she did. "You're not…" Then she lost the thought in panic and had to substitute an inadequate "Who are you?"

"Oh, don't be ridiculous, or worse yet, boring. You're too smart to ask stupid questions. You know who I am, just as surely as you know what I'm going to do to you."

One silent word repeated in Raven's head, and it wasn't polite. But it helped clear out some of the terror. "You're not Johnny Demars, but you're connected to him, and you're going to do what I assume you've been promising to do since you discovered that Aidan was alive. You're going to kill me and, like the soldier from the legend, have your revenge. An eye for an eye."

Chapter Sixteen

"I must have jiggled something loose when I fell." Gaitor played with his two-way as he and Aidan ran for the road. "Yours?"

"Stopped working after the last time I spoke to you."

"Do you have your cell?"

"It's in the Jeep—with Raven's. Come on, Gaitor, where did you park?"

"Point your flashlight east. You'll see the back end."

Panic threatened to spike, but Aidan found he could block it. The wicked thrust of love was another matter.

Picturing the gruesome possibilities had already slowed his thinking processes. Unable to shut them out completely, he used them to leap from thought to disconnected thought.

He'd left Raven with Fergus—but Demars was resourceful enough not to see that as an obstacle. There was a crowd of people on the ridge—but Weasel had plucked her out of a crowd, no problem.

Switch to something helpful, he ordered himself.

He could strike anyone he'd met or seen who was under forty-five from the list of potential crime lords. Ditto the people Gaitor referred to as the faithful. Take away Raven's distant relatives and Rooney's friends. Nix anyone else currently living in Raven's Cove.

That still left too many to count, and for all he knew, Demars hadn't made himself visible during his tenure here. His instincts argued that point, but as Gaitor had said more than once, instincts could be easily skewed by food, drink and intense emotions.

"Praise the Lord," his partner gasped when they finally reached the Jeep. He climbed in, panting. "Any brainstorms, yet?"

"No."

But he continued to bounce the possibilities as he shoved the vehicle in gear and swung out onto the road.

Gaitor wasn't quick enough to prevent the cassette recorder on the dash from hitting the floor. He picked it up. "Is this the machine you found in Weasel's pack, the one with the man's voice on it?"

"Yeah, but there's not enough on the tape to tell us anything."

Gaitor searched for the cassette that had fallen out. "I'll take a stab at it while you drive."

Although he nodded, Aidan's mind was no longer on the tape.

He'd felt the wrongness of tonight's pursuit from the start. Demars hadn't achieved his current level of success by doing the obvious. Guy Biggs, George's "big guy," had been a decoy. So had Phil Herron, though he'd likely had nothing to do with either Biggs or Demars. He'd been a dupe, and he'd died. Which told him that Johnny Demars possessed virtually no ethics at this juncture, and would murder without compunction or remorse.

Why in hell, a far distant part of his brain wondered, should that surprise him?

Voices from Weasel's recorder broke into the churn of his thoughts.

"You're turning him into your clone," a woman accused. "An adolescent Mini-Me."

"I'm giving him insight into a world which, until this moment, suited you very well."

Aidan frowned. "What is that?"

Gaitor nodded at the cassette recorder. "Tape fell out. I put it back in."

Although he was tempted to bang his head on the steering wheel for missing something as obvious as playing the flip side of Weasel's tape, Aidan settled for grinding his teeth and listening to the rest of the conversation.

"We're talking about a child, Johnny," the woman continued. "My child."

"Yours and mine," the man countered coldly. "This argument's old, and it's over. Jason is my future and the future of my business ventures. It ends here. He's not a toddler who needs his mother to coddle him. He's sixteen and more than capable of making his own choices. Now get out of my office. I have work to do."

"No."

One of them walked across the hard-surfaced floor.

"Get out," he repeated. "Now. Before my temper snaps."

"He's my child," the woman maintained.

"And mine."

Aidan heard it a second later, the unmistakable thwack of two silenced bullets. Two bullets that didn't ricochet or blast anything apart.

Something soft but solid hit the floor. Several seconds later, the feet moved again. This time, the steps were evenly spaced, the pace more deliberate. A deep breath heaved out.

And then the woman laughed.

JOANNE, RAVEN THOUGHT as panic clawed through her. The woman had said her name was Joanne. No surname given, none requested. Why bother when they'd been searching for a man.

"Walk," she barked now. "While you're at it, put your head mask back on. Better for me if no one sees you leaving the festivities."

Raven steadied her breathing. "Where are we going?"

"Far away from here. Make any sudden moves and know for a fact, Raven Blume, I'll kill you where you stand. Are we clear?"

"Perfectly." Keep her talking, Raven's terrified mind whispered. "Is your name really Joanne?"

"You want to chat, do you?" The woman shrugged. "Well, why not? Yes, my name's Joanne—Demars née Farber." She poked the gun hard into Raven's side. "You deduced the Demars part, I trust."

"It made sense. A mother avenging her child's death."

"Jason was murdered, Raven. Call a spade a spade."

She breathed in, then carefully out. "Where's your husband?"

Joanne laughed. "Ah, yes, my sweet, devoted, faceless Johnny. Sweet to no one, devoted to himself, faceless at the outset by choice and now because nature has the most amazing way of dealing with dead flesh. Oh, but I don't need to tell you that, do I, as you're a doctor and would know all about the process of decomposition." She gave a pleasurable sigh. "I planted him in the garden, under my petunias. Lovely flowers, a veritable riot of color every year. And you know, I've never added so much as a speck of fertilizer to the soil."

A shudder ran through Raven's body, but she kept her voice calm. "Did he die naturally, or did you kill him?"

"That would depend, I suppose, on how natural you

consider a bullet—no, sorry, two bullets—to the skull to be."

"About as natural as it was in Phil Herron's case."

"Herron was an irritant and an idiot. He tried to force himself on me physically." She snorted. "As if."

With the sound of the Reenactment fading, night sounds took over. The roar of the ocean, animals in the woods, the occasional whistle of wind.

Taking a chance, Raven slid her right arm from the sleeve of her cloak. Her two-way had been working earlier. Maybe she could play with the wires and make it work again.

To cover her movements, she kept the conversation going. "Would you have killed Herron if he hadn't forced himself on you?"

"Oh, come now, Raven. You don't give a rat's furry ass about Herron. What you really want to know is, do I kill for pleasure. The answer in general is no. Unfortunately, a death was necessary here, and Herron simply fit the bill. It was imperative that you and your hubby be properly deceived."

"So you did send a second shooter to the Cove. He just wasn't Phil Herron."

"Herron was an abrasive boob, nothing more. My second man was—and I trust still is—Guy Biggs. You know him. Small, wiry man with a long, gray braid and beard. Loves to mix fruit and alcohol in Mason jars. He slipped you the three feathers I'm sure you found in your pocket earlier. I thought it seemed fitting somehow. I warned Guy, via a text message, that he might wind up injured tonight. However, odds were no one would shoot to kill. Too many questions left unanswered that way. No, he'd be wanted alive. So I made him an offer he couldn't refuse. A little pain in return for an offensively large payoff."

"And the possibility of a prison sentence didn't factor in there anywhere?"

"No," Joanne said, and slid the gun up Raven's spine, "it didn't. Anyone can be gotten out of a hospital. And on the off chance he remains injury-free—well, let's say county jails are no more difficult to infiltrate than medical facilities."

Was she insane, Raven wondered, or merely viciously cruel? Maybe she was both. Fighting the fear that made her stomach knot and her fingers stiff, she kept working the wires and buttons on her radio. If she was very, very lucky Aidan might hear them talking and find her.

Where, though? Find her where?

"Where are you taking me?" she asked again.

"To the far side of Raven's Ridge." Joanne chuckled, and the sound was more chilling than her initial threat. "I considered simply putting a bullet in you and tossing you onto the rocks below, but that seemed anticlimactic somehow. Oh, Aidan would find your body one way or another, sooner or later, and he'd suffer when he did, but the shock value wouldn't be there, and I want that. I want to see his face when I blast yours off."

Raven's skin went clammy beneath her cloak. "He'll find a way to kill you, Joanne. If you know anything about him, you must know that."

"Did I mention I'll be shooting you from the distant shadows, at night, with a silenced bullet? It's been— tricky, what with anonymity needing to be maintained, but I've gotten Guy to teach me the ins and outs of using a rifle. It'll never be my weapon of choice, but if I say so myself, I've become rather proficient in the handling of one."

The mist thickened as they made their way to the more desolate portion of the ridge. Raven was tempted to scream, because—well, why not scream at this point? There was no one in the vicinity except her and Joanne Demars. Maybe a sudden shrill sound would startle the woman long enough for her to knock the gun away.

Another chuckle reached her. "Oh, Raven, I can hear your mind working as clearly as if you were speaking the words. You think you can throw me off my guard and get hold of my gun. But you're hampered by that cloak you're wearing, and given that your husband murdered my only son, I have an extremely eager trigger finger."

Raven heard the venom at the end of her statement, the bitterness and the hatred. But she heard no sorrow and wondered how deeply Joanne must have buried her grief in order to continue running her husband's criminal operation.

They'd reached the ruins of the west wing, and were heading for the jut of ridge directly behind Blume House. The thunder of drums and horns was far behind them now, and the spotlights were a mere glow of gold above the tree line. Even the woodland sounds were gone. There was only their feet on the rocks, and tendrils of white mist slinking like snakes around the boulders.

"You've gone strangely quiet, Raven, for a woman who's about to meet her maker."

"I've been—thinking," Raven lied, "about how I would feel and what I might do if my only child had died the way Jason did. Maybe I'd bring the person I felt responsible to a desolate ridge and throw him or her over the edge in the shadow of a haunted house, too."

"My, but you are a Blume, aren't you? Such a theatrical mind. If you think for one minute I'm emulating the actions of a certain WWI soldier, you're wrong. The setting simply suits my purpose. When we get to the lonely part of the ridge, I'll contact your husband and have my revenge. My closure."

What could she say? Raven thought. Except... "Did you know Weasel had a tape with your son's voice on it? We found it in his backpack. It sounded like Jason was talking on the phone. We assumed he was having a conversation with your husband, but I realize now, he was talking to you."

As she'd hoped, Joanne drew an annoyed breath through her nose. "Jason and I fought over Johnny's death many times. I wasn't aware back then that he'd recorded any of our fights."

"He sounded angry."

"He was angry, and so absolutely certain I'd killed his father that I thought he must have been hiding in the office that night and seen me do it. He repeated enough of the argument between Johnny and me that there could be no doubt he'd overheard us. But of course I understand now that his knowledge came from that cassette player of his. State-of-the-art was Johnny's way, the newer the better. But Jason wasn't like that. He loved electronic gadgets from any era. Still, it's of no consequence in the end. However Weasel acquired the thing, he's gone and so is his pathetic attempt at blackmail."

"Is that why you killed him? Because he tried to blackmail you?"

"He said he knew who I was and what I'd done. He insisted he'd discovered proof of my misdeeds. The fool actually texted me to gloat. And here's the astonishing thing. He wrote that text message while he was standing outside my food truck. I saw him hit Send. Then he laughed and ordered a raven burger with everything on it. From me.

"He signed his own death warrant then and there. He

merely speeded it up when he disobeyed my orders and decided to have a little extracurricular fun with you. I don't think he was as certain as he pretended to be, or if he was, that he would have done anything about it when he was sober. But he stole one of Guy's famous Mason jars and consumed a little more of the contents than was wise. He was intoxicated when he sent that text and labeled himself a blackmailer. I didn't need the problem he'd suddenly become. So I had Guy sic your husband on him—inasmuch as he could—then, when the opportunity arose, I eliminated him."

She gave the gun a nasty twist in Raven's back. Which hurt and caused her to twitch away from the tip. "What? Do you expect me to thank you for shooting him?"

Joanne's laugh echoed across the ridge. "You're feeling cranky and I understand that, but to answer your question, you should indeed thank me. Because, like Guy, Weasel had a fondness for sharp knives and soft female flesh. And whatever was going on in that sick brain of his, I don't believe he thought for one minute that I was on his little rodent tail the moment he left the crypt to find you. Oh, the delightful irony of good timing. Or bad timing in Weasel's case."

The edge of the ridge came into view ahead of them. Blume House stood dark and daunting in the background. Beneath her voluminous cloak, Raven kept pressing buttons on her two-way.

A velvety purr emerged from Joanne's throat as she stroked her gun along Raven's spine. "I can only imagine the prayers that must be whizzing around in your head, Raven dear. You want Aidan to come and save you. Well, you'll get half your wish at any rate. As you see, we've almost reached our destination. Once we're at the edge,

I'll call him. All I have to do then is give you one tiny shove if he steps a foot out of line."

Raven judged the remaining distance as they walked. Fifty, forty, thirty feet to the rim of the cliff.

Huge boulders, several of them shaped like malformed ravens, rose up around them. *Please God, please,* she prayed, *let Aidan come. But don't let him die trying to rescue me.*

Joanne's voice cut in again. "You can take off your mask now. We're well past the point where anyone will spot us."

The gun jabbed her ribs as Raven carefully slid her right hand back into the sleeve of her cloak and removed her head mask with her left.

"Perfect. Your pretty face is exposed and waiting for me to blow it away. Shall we make the call and bring..." A slight scuff on the rocks had her breaking off to demand, "Who's there?" Her foot came down on the trailing hem of Raven's cloak and stopped her progress. "Let me see who you are, or she gets a bullet that'll have her screaming in agony. Shall I elaborate?"

To Raven's shock—and horror—Gaitor emerged wearing his Reverend Alley disguise. He let the book he'd been holding drop to the ground as he slowly raised his hands.

"You!" Joanne exclaimed. "The oh-so-annoying preacher man. Didn't you like the answers I gave you this afternoon, Reverend?" She mocked her own response. "No, of course I didn't mean to implicate you in Phil Herron's death...." Her laugh was a brittle, tinkling sound in the cool night air. "Over there, old man. The Reenactment might not have been to your liking, but perhaps you'll enjoy the real thing. This woman's husband murdered my son. My child. My only child!"

Gaitor stood unmoving while Joanne went from icy laughter to virulent fury. Ahead of them, Raven saw what her captor apparently didn't—a movement near one of the bird-shaped boulders.

Her breath emerged in a silent rush of relief. And fear.

The relief was short lived as Joanne bunched the long cloak in her free hand and pushed the gun so far into Raven's side she was surprised it didn't puncture a kidney.

"I have three-quarter pressure on this trigger, my dear. If you so much as twitch, you'll be as dead as your raven man ancestor. Keep those hands up, preacher man, or you'll go before her. Now, here, take this." Joanne threw a small pack she'd been carrying to the ground. "Raven, you stand on that protrusion. Preacher, you pull the rope out of that bag and tie her up like a Thanksgiving turkey." She released Raven's cloak to draw a second gun from her jacket pocket. Pointing it at Gaitor's head, she said, "Get to work, Reverend. Now!"

Raven glanced at the boulder, but nothing stirred in the shadows behind Gaitor. Then she spotted the movement again and felt her stomach jitter.

Her heart stopped beating when she realized Joanne had seen it, as well.

Ducking smoothly behind Raven, she gave a silky laugh. "Oh, this is rich. He's here and I didn't even have to call him. My moment of triumph isn't quite as I envisioned it, but if there's one thing I am, it's adaptable." Her voice rose. "My gun, Lieutenant McInnis, is currently thrust against your wife's neck. That makes the range point-blank, and I have a frightening amount of pressure on the trigger. The only shot you've got is through her. I want your weapons on the ground where I can see them, and your hands high in the air."

Two guns landed on the rock. A second later, Aidan emerged, dressed as a raven.

"Interesting choice of attire," Joanne acknowledged. "Keep those hands way up, McInnis. Move it with the ropes, old man."

Raven's heart pounded as terror streaked through her. She didn't doubt for a minute that the trigger was more than half squeezed. Maybe Aidan could do something, but not before the gun went off, killing her and probably Gaitor, as well.

Gaitor finished securing the knot around her ankles. When he gave the rope an extra tug, Raven lowered her eyes.

And widened them in astonishment.

"Very good, old man," Joanne congratulated. "Now stand and hobble over to the raven, who's going to—"

The movement was so fast Raven missed it. With no warning, she was knocked away from the edge of the cliff. The gun disappeared from her neck. Although stunned by the sudden motion, she immediately began struggling with her bonds.

Gloved hands appeared to help her and she stared into the eyes of the raven's-head mask. "Gotta get you out of here." Gaitor's voice came from behind it.

The moment he'd freed her wrists, she shed the ropes around her ankles, then brought her head around as a gun went off behind them—once, twice, three times.

She scrambled to her feet. "Aidan's unarmed, Gaitor. I won't leave him here alone."

"He's not unarmed… Wait! Raven, come back! I'm the one who threw down my weapons."

She heard him. She also knew that Aidan was too good to ever be weaponless. But the reverend's long coat wouldn't be as easy to shuck off as her cloak. And bottom line? She had no idea who'd fired those three shots.

She was running past a huddled rock formation when a pair of hands came out to haul her in.

She fought automatically and only stopped when she recognized the hiss of pain.

"Aidan?" On her knees, Raven took his now-beardless face in her hands. "Thank God, you're all right."

"Not sure I'd go that far," he replied. "Don't ask," he said before she could. "I don't know where she is, or I'd tell you to get the hell away from here."

Raven looked around but saw nothing. "She has a rifle stashed somewhere up here. Her plan was to get you to come up to this part of the ridge so she could kill me in front of you. She specifically said she wanted to see your face when she blew mine off."

"Yeah, well, we'll see whose face gets blown off."

Raven started to speak, but choked the words back when he pushed her to the ground.

A moment later, the ridge exploded with light and sound. Raven heard gunshots, possibly rifle shots and a cacophony of other noises she couldn't identify.

When she finally got her head up, Aidan was using his Glock, while above them, a dazzling display of fireworks illuminated the night sky. Much lower to the ground, the top of the rock formation blew apart, so, yes, she had indeed heard rifle shots.

"Where is she?" Raven yelled.

"She's moving," Aidan shouted back. He used his two-way. "Gaitor, can you pinpoint Joanne's location…? Gaitor?"

Raven's eyes landed on a pair of feet sticking out from behind a boulder. "Aidan, he's hurt!"

"Stay behind me." He waited through another round of shots, then tapped her hip. "Okay, head for the boulder."

Raven stayed low and ran. High above them, starbursts of gold, red and silver rained down. When she reached the misshapen rock, she went to her knees beside the older man. Thank God, the pulse in his neck was strong and steady. "Gaitor, can you hear me?"

A hand came out of the darkness. Cruel fingers sank into Raven's hair and wrenched her sideways half a second before Aidan appeared.

"Nice try, ace, but as I've told you many times, my son's dead, therefore, Raven's dead. Move one muscle, Lieutenant, and her brain leaves her body in bloody bits."

The tip of her gun pressed into Raven's temple. She looked up at Aidan, who tossed his Glock and raised his palms in an outward show of surrender.

"Very good," Joanne's voice tightened. "Now get up, Raven. We're exactly where we need to be for this little drama of mine to play out. Who knows, maybe we're exactly where the soldier from your legend murdered his friend on the rocks below."

With a gun to her head, Raven had no choice but to comply. That didn't mean she had to make it easy for the woman holding it. She kept her eyes on Aidan, saw his faint nod and held herself perfectly still.

Fireworks continued to rain down on the other side of the ridge. She had to step over Gaitor's prone body to reach the ledge that protruded over the wild ocean waves. Drawing a deep breath, Raven deliberately stumbled on the older man's legs.

Because her hand was now firmly clamped to Raven's arm, Joanne stumbled with her. Off balance and momentarily startled, the woman's grip faltered. In that split second, Raven got her elbow up to knock the gun aside.

She saw Aidan's lightning-fast reaction but doubted she would ever know how he got his backup out so quickly.

"Don't," he warned, when Joanne would have swung her arm back. "Let her go." He extended a hand. "Raven?"

Although she hated to leave Gaitor, Raven worked herself free of the woman's grip and started toward him.

Joanne stood, a statue in black spandex with her back to the crashing waves and the glittering explosions overhead.

"Drop the gun, and come away from the edge," Aidan told her.

They both saw her smile.

"Go to hell," she replied, and, snapping her hand down, took aim at Raven's head.

A single shot rang out between starbursts.

For a frozen moment, Raven thought whoever had fired must have missed. Then Joanne's arm dropped, her eyes opened a fraction wider, and, taking one staggering step backward, she plunged over the side of the cliff.

Unbelieving, Raven stared—so long and hard she almost tumbled into the water herself. But Aidan's arm around her torso drew her firmly back.

"I don't think so, sweetheart." Sliding his other arm around her, he set his cheek against hers. "Danger's gone. Look up instead of down."

Still too shocked to speak, Raven raised her eyes to the sky. For a heartbeat of time, the mist vanished. In that moment, she spied the glittering outline of an enormous raven. It hung over the ridge, until, slowly, slowly, the wings began to fold in on themselves.

One by one, the sparkles winked out. In a matter of seconds, all that remained were two red eyes staring into the blackened ocean waves that slammed against the base of Raven's Ridge.

Epilogue

The remainder of the night passed like a fragmented dream.

Revived and relatively uninjured, Gaitor was disgusted with himself. After days of surviving the perils of his ankle-length coat, his first attempt to run in a raven's cloak had resulted in him tripping on the hem and plowing headfirst into a rock.

"Knocked myself out cold," he said from his freshly made bed at Blume House. "Thankfully, I don't have to answer to anyone for my clumsiness."

Although she examined him for signs of concussion, Raven found nothing and in the end let Rooney take a pot of tea and two large mugs upstairs for a visit. By morning, she imagined her great-grandfather would have concocted a new and greatly embellished version of the night's events.

"The Ravenspellers are eating this up," Steven relayed during one of many passes through the great hall. "I'm starting to think we, as a community, are not making the most of our family's history. If any of what Rooney says is to be believed, there are all manner of addendums to the original Hezekiah legend. 'The Soldier's Tale' is the tip of the iceberg."

At last, Raven thought, the light was back in her cousin's eyes. True, it had a mercenary tinge, but for a disbarred lawyer, purpose was paramount, and apparently Steven had found one that appealed.

As for Aidan... Inasmuch as she loved and believed in him, he still had a great deal of explaining to do about last night. However, with no town authority present in the Cove, it was left to him and the county deputies to fill in. That included the filing of assault, kidnapping and attempted murder charges against Guy Biggs. When foggy daylight returned, it also entailed the unpleasant task of searching the rocks and indentations under Raven's Ridge for the body of Joanne Demars.

As the first light of morning pearled the sky, Raven showered and dressed. She borrowed coffee from Aidan's stash in the attic, brewed a pot of dark roast, then hunted up two travel mugs and headed for the beach.

"I love you more than life itself," Aidan said when he saw her.

Laughing, Raven handed him a steaming mug. "Back at you, Lieutenant. But you'd say that to anyone who brought you coffee at the crack of dawn."

"I wouldn't mean it, though." Curling his fingers around her neck, he set his mouth on hers for a very long, very thorough kiss. "How's life up at Blume House?"

When her head cleared, she smiled. "Oh, you know, same old, same old. Poor Fergus is moping around like a lost and mournful soul."

"He feels guilty for not guarding you properly after Gaitor and I left the ridge."

"I appreciate the sentiment, but as I've told him a hundred times, if he hadn't left on his own, Joanne might have shot him."

Aidan drank a mouthful of coffee. "Not might, Raven. She'd have killed him without compunction. She emulated her husband's style in order to maintain the facade, but, beyond the mother-child connection, I didn't sense much feeling in her."

"Guess we have something to thank Johnny for, after all."

Dropping an arm over her shoulders, Aidan tapped his mug to hers. "Here's to Johnny and maintaining the illusion."

She sent him a humorous look. "Speaking of illusions, it was very clever of you to switch disguises with Gaitor and become Reverend Alley yourself. Your idea?"

"More or less. I heard snatches of your conversation with Joanne on my radio while Gaitor and I were heading back to the Ravenspell site. A switch seemed like the way to go."

Raven kissed his cheek. "You're such a good cop, Aidan, and an even better husband. Did you hear the part of our conversation where Joanne admitted to murdering Johnny?"

"Yeah, I heard it. But not as part of her talk with you. The fatal conversation, if you can call it that, between Joanne and Johnny is on the flip side of the mini cassette Weasel stole from wherever he stole it from. Jason's possessions as they were being packed away, I imagine. Obviously, Jason was talking to his mother on the side of the tape we all heard."

"And the man who said his name at the end?"

"My guess would be Johnny. Jason probably taped over an old conversation he'd had with his father. His name was there from an older recording."

Raven's gaze touched on the white-capped waves that broke against the rocks with a foamy vengeance. "I don't know about Johnny, but I do think Joanne really loved her son. Why else would she have been so determined to make you pay for taking him away from her?"

"Joanne was obsessed, Raven, and she let that obsession eat her up. We didn't get much out of Biggs, but he did tell us that she was furious when she heard I'd died in an explosion."

"Furious enough to come to your wake, apparently. She posed as one of the caterers. I finally put the two faces together—the server who'd been trying to get me to eat a smoked salmon canapé with the raven dog lady in the silver truck."

"Aidan, Raven! Over here!" A fisherman waved his arm. "We found her. She's pretty bashed up."

"Lovely." Raven made herself walk with Aidan toward the water. "Always fun to view a bashed-up corpse before breakfast."

"Better before than after. Are you sure you want to see her?"

"Sad to say, I need to."

But she had to admit, Raven thought afterward, the grisly image wasn't one she'd forget any time soon.

She watched from a high beach rock as Joanne's body was prepped for its journey to the county morgue.

"You know, I'm really glad I didn't choose forensic medicine," she admitted to Aidan. Looking up, she visualized the starburst raven they'd seen last night. "You told the organizers to start the fireworks ahead of schedule, didn't you?"

"As distractions go, it seemed like a good one." He settled behind her, let her lean back into his chest. "So what now, angel? Do we move to Raven's Cove, lock, stock and China barrel—you as town medic and me in some kind of law enforcement position?"

She smiled. "I've been giving that question a great deal

of thought. It's true, Raven's Cove needs a clinic, and I'll be happy to help set one up, but I contacted a colleague at Mayo and one of his associates is looking to relocate to a small town. He's fifty-one, he earned his medical degree in Germany and he worked as an army surgeon for the first ten years of his career. His name's Froy." Her eyes sparkled at Aidan's narrowed expression. "Froy, not Freud. Mind you, he does have a goatee beard, but his first name's Henrik."

"Okay, well that still leaves us with a choice. Rochester or Milwaukee?"

She shook her head. "Honestly? I'm so happy you're alive, I don't care where we live."

"In that case, lets go with Rochester. I want to brag to my colleagues about my brainy wife."

"Yeah, right. Your wife who has a cursed ancestor she half believes she saw floating in the sky last night."

"You saw a pyrotechnic illusion, Raven."

She grinned. "You think that, and I think that, but Steven, who arranged for those pyrotechnics to be shipped, swore to me there was no red-eyed raven included in the order that he himself placed on Rooney's behalf six months ago." She arched a teasing brow. "Explain that one away, Lieutenant McInnis."

"I don't have to." Catching her chin, he ran his thumb over her bottom lip, then slowly lowered his mouth to hers. "As you said—it is Ravenspell, and we're in Raven's Cove, after all."

* * * * *

COMING NEXT MONTH from Harlequin® Intrigue®
AVAILABLE MARCH 19, 2013

#1413 CARDWELL RANCH TRESPASSER
B.J. Daniels

A stranger has entered Cardwell Ranch, and Hilde Jacobson is the only person who can see her for who she really is. Risking her own life—and heart—she joins forces with the only man she can trust, Deputy Marshal Colt Dawson.

#1414 SCENE OF THE CRIME: DEADMAN'S BLUFF
Carla Cassidy

When FBI agent Seth Hawkins takes a vacation the last thing he expects while riding some sand dunes is to find a live woman buried in the sand.

#1415 CONCEAL, PROTECT
Brothers in Arms: Fully Engaged
Carol Ericson

When Noelle Dupree escapes Washington, D.C., for some peace and solitude at her Colorado ranch, danger follows her. Can a sexy cowboy ease her fears, or will he bring mayhem to her doorstep...and her heart?

#1416 STAR WITNESS
The Delancey Dynasty
Mallory Kane

If Harte and Dani can trust each other enough to survive a killer storm and a deadly chase, one night will be enough to forge a lasting love.

#1417 ROYAL RESCUE
Royal Bodyguards
Lisa Childs

For three years FBI agent Brendan O'Hannigan thought Josie Jessup dead. To keep both her and the son he didn't know about alive, he'll willingly give up his own life.

#1418 SECURE LOCATION
The Detectives
Beverly Long

Detective Cruz Montoya has one chance to save his ex-wife and their unborn child...but will old secrets get in the way?

You can find more information on upcoming Harlequin® titles, free excerpts and more at www.Harlequin.com.

HICNM0313

REQUEST YOUR FREE BOOKS!
2 FREE NOVELS PLUS 2 FREE GIFTS!

❖ HARLEQUIN®

INTRIGUE®

BREATHTAKING ROMANTIC SUSPENSE

YES! Please send me 2 FREE Harlequin Intrigue® novels and my 2 FREE gifts (gifts are worth about $10). After receiving them, if I don't wish to receive any more books, I can return the shipping statement marked "cancel." If I don't cancel, I will receive 6 brand-new novels every month and be billed just $4.49 per book in the U.S. or $5.24 per book in Canada. That's a savings of at least 14% off the cover price! It's quite a bargain! Shipping and handling is just 50¢ per book in the U.S. and 75¢ per book in Canada.* I understand that accepting the 2 free books and gifts places me under no obligation to buy anything. I can always return a shipment and cancel at any time. Even if I never buy another book, the two free books and gifts are mine to keep forever.

182/382 HDN FVQV

Name _____ (PLEASE PRINT)

Address _____ Apt. #

City _____ State/Prov. _____ Zip/Postal Code

Signature (if under 18, a parent or guardian must sign)

Mail to the **Harlequin® Reader Service:**
IN U.S.A.: P.O. Box 1867, Buffalo, NY 14240-1867
IN CANADA: P.O. Box 609, Fort Erie, Ontario L2A 5X3

**Are you a subscriber to Harlequin Intrigue books
and want to receive the larger-print edition?
Call 1-800-873-8635 or visit www.ReaderService.com.**

* Terms and prices subject to change without notice. Prices do not include applicable taxes. Sales tax applicable in N.Y. Canadian residents will be charged applicable taxes. Offer not valid in Quebec. This offer is limited to one order per household. Not valid for current subscribers to Harlequin Intrigue books. All orders subject to credit approval. Credit or debit balances in a customer's account(s) may be offset by any other outstanding balance owed by or to the customer. Please allow 4 to 6 weeks for delivery. Offer available while quantities last.

Your Privacy—The Harlequin® Reader Service is committed to protecting your privacy. Our Privacy Policy is available online at www.ReaderService.com or upon request from the Harlequin Reader Service.

We make a portion of our mailing list available to reputable third parties that offer products we believe may interest you. If you prefer that we not exchange your name with third parties, or if you wish to clarify or modify your communication preferences, please visit us at www.ReaderService.com/consumerschoice or write to us at Harlequin Reader Service Preference Service, P.O. Box 9062, Buffalo, NY 14269. Include your complete name and address.

HI13

Colt saw that she had a stunned look on her face. Stunned and disappointed. It was heartbreaking.

Without a word, he took her in his arms. Hilde was trembling. He took her over to the couch, then went to her liquor cabinet and found some bourbon. He poured her a couple fingers worth.

"Drink this," he said.

"Aren't you afraid what I might do liquored up?" she asked sarcastically.

"Terrified," he said, and stood over her until she'd downed every drop. "You want to talk about it?" he asked, taking the empty glass from her and joining her on the couch.

She let out a laugh. "*I* hardly believe what happened. Why would I expect anyone else to?"

"I believe you. I believe everything you've told me."

Tears welled in her brown eyes. He drew her to him and kissed her, holding her tightly. "I'm sorry you had to go through this alone."

She nodded and wiped hastily at the tears as she drew back to look at him. "You're my only hope right now. We have to find out everything we can about this woman." And then she told him everything, from finding the shop vandalized to what led up to her being nearly arrested.

When she finished, he said, "We shouldn't be surprised."

"Surprised? I'm still in shock. To do something like that to yourself…"

"You knew Dee was sick."

Hilde nodded. "What will she do next? That's what worries me."

Colt didn't want to say it, but that's what worried him. "Maybe Hud has the right idea. Isn't there somewhere—"

"I'm not leaving. Dee told me that I've never had to fight for anything. Well, I'm fighting now. I'm bringing her down. One way or another."

"Hilde—"

"She has to be stopped."

"I agree. But we have to be careful. She's dangerous." He felt his phone vibrate, checked it and saw that his boss had sent him a text. "Hud wants to see me ASAP." Not good. "I don't want to leave you here alone."

"I'll be fine. Dee won this round. She won't do anything for a while and I'm not going to give her another chance to use me like she did today."

He heard the courage, as well as the determination, in her voice. Hilde was strong and, no matter what Dee had told her, she *was* a fighter.

*Can Hilde and Colt stop Dee's deadly plan
before it's too late?*

*Find out what happens next in
CARDWELL RANCH TRESPASSER. Available March 19
from Harlequin Intrigue!*